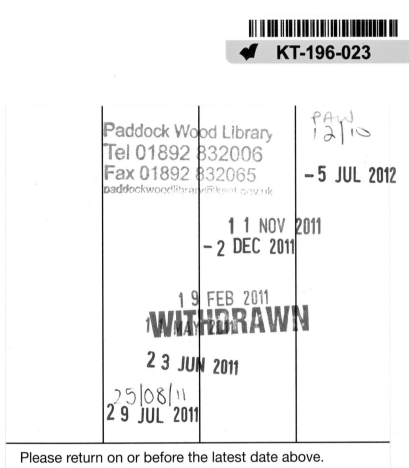
Please return on or before the latest date above.
You can renew online at *www.kent.gov.uk/libs*
or by telephone 08458 247 200

H9.

THE FIRST MAN YOU MEET

THE FIRST MAN YOU MEET

DEBBIE MACOMBER

THORNDIKE
CHIVERS

This Large Print edition is published by Thorndike Press, Waterville, Maine, USA and by BBC Audiobooks Ltd, Bath, England.
Thorndike Press, a part of Gale, Cengage Learning.

The text of this Large Print edition is unabridged.
Other aspects of the book may vary from the original edition.
Set in 16 pt. Plantin.

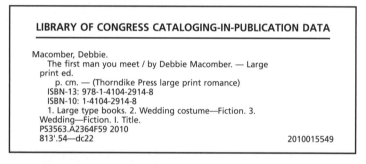

LIBRARY OF CONGRESS CATALOGING-IN-PUBLICATION DATA

Macomber, Debbie.
  The first man you meet / by Debbie Macomber. — Large print ed.
    p. cm. — (Thorndike Press large print romance)
    ISBN-13: 978-1-4104-2914-8
    ISBN-10: 1-4104-2914-8
    1. Large type books. 2. Wedding costume—Fiction. 3. Wedding—Fiction. I. Title.
PS3563.A2364F59 2010
813'.54—dc22   2010015549

BRITISH LIBRARY CATALOGUING-IN-PUBLICATION DATA AVAILABLE

Published in 2010 in the U.S. by arrangement with Harlequin Books S.A.
Published in 2010 in the U.K. by arrangement with Harlequin Enterprises II B.V.

U.K. Hardcover: 978 1 408 49241 3 (Chivers Large Print)
U.K. Softcover: 978 1 408 49242 0 (Camden Large Print)

Printed in the United States of America
1 2 3 4 5 6 7 14 13 12 11 10

For James Jordan Buckley,
the other writer in the family.

ONE

It had been one of those days.

One of those nightmarish days in which nothing had gone right. Nothing. Shelly Hansen told herself she should have seen the writing on the wall that morning when she tripped over the laces of her high-top purple running shoes as she hurried from the parking lot to her dinky office. She'd torn a hole in the knee of her brand-new pants and limped ingloriously into her building. The day had gone steadily downhill from there, with a package lost by the courier and — worst of all — the discovery that her bank account was overdrawn because a client's check had bounced.

By the time she returned to her apartment that evening she was in a black mood. All she needed to make her day complete was to have her mother pop in unannounced with a man in tow, convinced she'd found the perfect mate for Shelly.

She could only hope that wouldn't happen, but it was exactly the kind of thing Shelly had come to expect from her dear, sweet *desperate* mother. Shelly was twenty-eight now and still single, and her mother tended to view her unmarried status as a situation to be remedied. Since her father had decided not to retire, and her two brothers were both living out of state, Shelly had become the focus of her mother's obsessions. Marriage, closely followed by grandchildren, were the first and second items on Faith Hansen's agenda for her only daughter.

Never mind that Shelly felt content with her life just the way it was. Never mind that she wasn't interested in marriage and children . . . at least not yet. That time would come, she was sure, not now, but someday soon — or rather, some *year* soon.

For the moment, Shelly was absorbed in her career. She was proud of her work as a video producer, although she continually suffered the cash-flow problems of the self-employed. Her relaxation DVDs — seascapes, mountain scenes, a flickering fire in a brick fireplace, all with a background of classical music — were selling well. Her cat-sitting DVD had recently caught the attention of a major distributor, and she couldn't help believing she was on the brink of real success.

That was the good news.

Her mother hounding her to get married was the bad.

Tossing her woven Mexican bag and striped blue jacket onto the sofa, Shelly ventured into the kitchen and sorted through the packages in her freezer until she found something that halfway appealed to her for dinner. The frozen entrée was in the microwave when the doorbell chimed.

Her mother. The way her day was going, it *had* to be her mother. Groaning inwardly, she decided she'd be polite but insistent. Friendly but determined, and if her mother began talking about husbands, Shelly would simply change the subject.

But it wasn't Faith Hansen who stood outside her door. It was Elvira Livingston, the building manager, a warm, delightful but insatiably curious older woman.

"Good evening, dear," Mrs. Livingston greeted her. She wore heavy gold earrings and a billowing, bright yellow dress, quite typical attire. She clutched a large box protectively in both hands. "The postman dropped this off. He asked if I'd give it to you."

"For me, Mrs. L.?" Perhaps today wasn't

a total loss, after all.

Elvira nodded, holding the package as though she wasn't entirely sure she should surrender it until she got every bit of relevant data. "The return address is California. Know anyone by the name of Millicent Bannister?"

"Aunt Milly?" Shelly hadn't heard from her mother's aunt in years.

"The package is insured," Mrs. Livingston noted, shifting the box just enough to examine the label again.

Shelly held out her hands to receive the package, but her landlady apparently didn't notice.

"I had to sign for it." This, too, seemed to be of great importance. "And there's a letter attached," Mrs. Livingston added.

Shelly had the impression that the only way she'd ever get her hands on the parcel was to let Mrs. Livingston open it first.

"I certainly appreciate all the trouble you've gone to," Shelly said, gripping the sides of the box and giving a firm tug. Mrs. Livingston released the package reluctantly. "Uh, thanks, Mrs. L. I'll talk to you soon."

The older woman's face fell with disappointment as Shelly began to close the door. Obviously, she was hoping for an invitation to stay. But Shelly wasn't in the mood for company, especially not the meddlesome, if well-meaning, Elvira Livingston.

Shelly sighed. This was what she got for renting an apartment with "character." She could be living in a modern town house with a sauna, pool and workout room in a suburban neighborhood. Instead she'd opted for a brick two-story apartment building in the heart of Seattle. The radiators hissed at all hours of the night in perfect harmony with the plumbing that groaned and creaked. But Shelly loved the polished hardwood floors, the high ceilings with their delicate crystal light fixtures and the bay windows that overlooked Puget Sound. She could do without the sauna and other amenities, even if it meant occasionally dealing with an eccentric busybody like Mrs. Livingston.

Eagerly she carried the package into the kitchen and set it on her table. Although she wondered what Aunt Milly had sent her, she carefully peeled the letter free, then just as carefully removed the plain brown wrapper.

The box was an old one, she noticed, the cardboard heavier than that currently used by stores. Shelly gently pried off the lid. She found layers of tissue paper wrapped around . . . a dress. Shelly pushed aside the

11

paper and lifted the garment from its box. She gasped in surprise as the long white dress gracefully unfolded.

This wasn't just any dress. It was a wedding dress, an exquisitely sewn lace-and-satin wedding dress.

Surely it couldn't have been Aunt Milly's . . . No, that couldn't be . . . It wasn't possible.

Anxious now, her heart racing, Shelly refolded the dress and placed it back in the box. She reached for the envelope and saw that her hands were trembling as she tore it open.

My Dearest Shelly,

I trust this letter finds you happy and well. You've frequently been in my thoughts the past few days. I suppose you could blame Dr. Phil for that. Though now that I think about it, it may have been Oprah. As you'll have gathered, I often watch those talk shows these days. John would have disapproved, but he's been gone eight years now. Of course, if I wanted to, I'd watch them if he were still alive. John could disapprove all he wanted, but it wouldn't do him a bit of good. Never did. He knew it and loved me, anyway.

I imagine you're wondering why I'm mailing you my wedding dress and what Dr. Phil and Oprah have to do with it. (Yes, that is indeed my infamous wedding dress.) I suspect the sight of it has put the fear of God into you. I wish I could've been there to see your face when you realized what I was sending you. No doubt you're familiar with the story; everyone in the family's known about it for years. Since you're fated to marry the first man you meet once the dress is in your hands, your instinct is probably to burn the thing immediately!

Now that I reconsider, I'm certain it was Dr. Phil. He had a show recently featuring pets as companions to the elderly, lifting their spirits and the like. The man being interviewed brought along a cute little Scottish terrier and that was when the old seamstress drifted into my mind. Her name was Mrs. McDonald — or was it McDonnell? At any rate, I must have fallen asleep, because the next thing I knew the six-o'clock news was on.

While I slept I had a dream about you. This was no ordinary dream, either. I saw you plain as day, standing beside a tall young man, your blue eyes bright and shining. You were so happy, so truly in love. But what astonished me was the wedding dress you were wearing.

Mine.

The very dress the old Scottish woman sewed for me all those years ago. It seemed to me I was receiving a message of some sort and that I'd best not ignore it. Neither should you! You're about to embark on the grandest adventure of your life, my dear. Keep me informed!

Believe me, Shelly, I know what you're thinking. I well remember my own thoughts the day that seamstress handed me the wedding dress. I'd ordered something completely different from her — a simple evening gown — so I was shocked to say the least. Marriage was the *last* thing on my mind! I had a career, back in the days when it was rare for a woman to attend college, let alone graduate from law school.

You and I are a great deal alike, Shelly. We value our independence. It takes a special kind of man to be married to women like us. And you, my dear niece, are about to meet that one special man just the way I did.

All my love,
Aunt Milly

P.S. You're only the second person to wear the dress. Never before have I felt anything like this. Perhaps it's the beginning of a new tradition!

With hands that trembled even more fiercely now, Shelly folded the letter and slid it back into the envelope. Her heart was pounding, and she could feel the sweat beading her forehead.

The phone rang then, and more from instinct than any desire to talk, Shelly picked up the receiver.

"Hello." It hadn't dawned on her until that moment that the caller might be her mother, wanting to bring over a man for her to meet. Any man her mother introduced would only add to the growing nightmare, but —

"Shelly, it's Jill. Are you all right? You sound . . . strange."

"Jill." Shelly was so relieved that her knees went weak. "Thank heaven it's you."

"What's wrong?"

Shelly hardly knew where to begin. "My aunt Milly's wedding dress just arrived. I realize that won't mean anything to you unless you've heard the family legend about my aunt Milly and uncle John."

"I haven't."

"Of course you haven't, otherwise you'd understand what I'm going through," Shelly snapped, then felt guilty for being short-tempered with her best friend. Making an effort to compose herself, she explained, "I've just been mailed a wedding dress — one that's been in my family for over sixty years — with the clear understanding that I'll be wearing it soon myself."

"You didn't even tell me you were dating anyone." Jill hadn't managed to disguise the hurt in her voice.

"I'm *not!* And I'm not getting married, either. If anyone should know that, it's you."

"Then your aunt intends you to wear it when you do get married."

"There's more to it than that," Shelly cried. "Listen. Aunt Milly — who's really my mother's aunt, a few years older than my grandmother — became an attorney just after the Second World War. She worked hard to earn her law degree and had decided to dedicate her life to her career."

"In other words, she'd planned never to marry."

"Exactly."

"But apparently she did."

"Yes, and the story of how that happened has been in the family for years. It seems Aunt Milly had all her clothes profession-

16

ally made. As the story goes, she took some lovely white material to an old Scottish woman who had a reputation as the best seamstress around. Milly needed an evening dress for some formal event that was coming up — business-related, of course. The woman took her measurements and told her the dress would be finished by the end of the week."

"And?" Jill prompted when Shelly hesitated.

"And . . . when Milly returned for the dress the old woman sat her down with a cup of tea."

"The dress wasn't ready?"

"Oh, it was ready, all right, only it wasn't the dress Aunt Milly had ordered. The Scottish woman said she was gifted with the 'sight.' "

"She was clairvoyant?"

"So she claimed," Shelly said, breathing in deeply. "The old woman told my aunt that when she began the dress a vision came to her. A clear vision that involved Milly. This vision showed Milly getting married. The old woman was so convinced of it that she turned what was supposed to be a simple evening dress into an elaborate wedding gown, with layers of satin and lace and lots of pearls."

"It sounds beautiful," Jill said with a sigh.

"Of course it's beautiful — but don't you see?"

"See what?"

It was all Shelly could do not to groan with frustration. "The woman insisted my aunt Milly would marry within the year. It happened, too, just the way that seamstress said, right down to the last detail."

Jill sighed again. "That's the most romantic story I've heard in ages."

"It isn't romance," Shelly argued, "it's fate interrupting one's life! It's being a . . . pawn! It's destiny whether you like it or not. I know that seems crazy, but I've grown up hearing this story. It was as though my aunt Milly didn't have any choice in the matter."

"And your aunt Milly mailed you the dress?"

"Yes," Shelly wailed. "*Now* do you understand why I'm upset?"

"Frankly, no. Come on, Shelly, it's just an old dress. You're overreacting. You make it sound as if you're going to marry the next man you meet."

Shelly gasped audibly. "How'd you know?" she whispered.

"Know what?"

"That's *exactly* what happened to Aunt Milly. That's part of the legend. She tried to refuse the dress, but the seamstress wouldn't take it back, nor would she accept payment. When Aunt Milly left the dress shop, she had car problems and needed a mechanic. My uncle John was that mechanic. And Aunt Milly married him. She married *the first man she met,* just like the seamstress said."

Two

"Shelly, that doesn't mean *you're* going to marry the next man you meet," Jill stated calmly, far too calmly to suit Shelly.

Perhaps Jill didn't recognize a crisis when she came across one. They were talking about fate here. Predestination. Okay, maybe, just maybe, she was being a bit melodramatic, but after the ghastly day she'd had, who could blame her?

"Aunt Milly came right out and said I'm going to get married soon," Shelly said. "According to the family legend, the first man you meet when you get the dress is the man you'll marry."

"It's just coincidence," Jill reassured her. "Your aunt probably would've met her husband *without* the dress. It would've happened anyway. And don't forget, she's an old woman now," Jill continued soothingly. "I know this wonderful old lady who comes into the pharmacy every few weeks and she always insists *I'm* going to get married soon. I smile and nod and fill her prescription. She means well, and I'm sure your aunt Milly does, too. She just wants you to be happy, the way she was. But I think it's silly to take any of this prediction nonsense seriously."

Shelly exhaled sharply. Jill was right; Aunt Milly was a lovely woman who had Shelly's happiness at heart. She'd had a long, blissful marriage herself and wanted the same for her great-niece. But Shelly had plans and goals, none of which included meeting and marrying a stranger.

The story of Aunt Milly's wedding dress had been handed down through the family. Shelly had first heard it as a child and had loved it. She'd ranked the story of her aunt Milly and uncle John with her favorite fairy tales of Cinderella and Sleeping Beauty, barely able to distinguish truth from fantasy. However, she was an adult now. Her heart and her life weren't going to be ruled by something as whimsical as a "magic" wedding dress or a fanciful legend.

"You're absolutely right," Shelly announced emphatically. "The whole thing is ridiculous. Just because this wedding dress supposedly conjured up a husband for my aunt Milly sixty-plus years ago doesn't

21

mean it's going to do the same thing for me, no matter what she claims."

"Well, thank goodness you're finally being sensible about this."

"No one bothered to ask me what I thought before shipping off a so-called magic wedding gown. I don't want to get married yet, so I certainly don't need the dress. It was a nice gesture, but unnecessary."

"Exactly," Jill agreed.

"I'm not interested in playing déjà voodoo." She paused to laugh at her own joke.

Jill chuckled, too. "I wouldn't be, either."

Shelly felt greatly relieved, and the tight muscles along the back of her neck began to relax. Jill was, as usual, full of practical advice. Aunt Milly was a wonderful old lady, and the legend was a delightful bit of family lore, but it would be laughable to take any of this seriously.

"How about meeting me for lunch tomorrow?" Jill suggested. "It's been ages since we got together."

"Sounds good to me," Shelly said. Although they'd been close friends since college, it took some effort on both their parts these days to make time in their hectic lives to see each other. "When and where?"

"How about the mall?" Jill asked. "That

would be easiest for me since I'm scheduled to work tomorrow. I can get off a few minutes before twelve."

"Great. I'll see you at noon at Patrick's," Shelly promised. Meeting her friend for lunch was just the antidote she needed after her terrible day. But what did she expect on Friday, April thirteenth?

Shelly overslept, then got stuck in a traffic jam on her way to meet Jill the following morning. She detested being late, although she often was. Rather than fight for a convenient parking spot in the vast lot that surrounded the mall, she took the first available space and rushed over to the nearest entrance. Patrick's, a cozy, charming restaurant on the mall's upper level, was deservedly popular for business lunches. Shelly had eaten there often and especially enjoyed the spinach-and-shrimp salad.

A glance at her watch told her it was already after twelve, and not wanting to keep Jill waiting, she hurried toward the escalator, weaving her way through the crowd.

Her mind must have been on the salad she intended to order instead of the escalator because the moment she placed her foot on the first tread, she lost her balance.

"Oh . . . oh!" Swinging both arms out in a futile attempt to remain upright, she groped at thin air. She tried frantically to catch herself as she fell backward.

Landing in someone's arms shocked her as much as having lost her balance. Incredulous, she twisted around to thank her rescuer but this proved to be a mistake. Her action caught the man off guard, and before he could prevent it, they went crashing to the floor. Once again Shelly expected to experience pain. Instead, her waist was surrounded by arms that were surprisingly strong. His grip was firm but gentle, protective. As they fell, he maneuvered himself to take the brunt of the impact when they landed. Sprawled as she was above him, Shelly found herself staring down at the most attractive man she'd ever seen. Her heart thrummed. Her breath caught. Her body froze.

For a moment neither of them spoke. A crowd had gathered around them before Shelly managed to speak. When she did, her voice was weak and breathless. "Are you all right? I'm so sorry . . ."

"I'm fine. What about you?"

"Fine. I think."

She lay cushioned by his solid chest, their faces mere inches apart. Shelly's long hair fell forward, framing his face. He smelled of mint and some clean-scented soap. Her gaze wandered curiously over his features; at such close range she could see the tiny lines that fanned out from the edges of his sapphire-blue eyes, as well as the grooves that bracketed his mouth. His nose was classically straight, his mouth full and sensuous. At least his lower lip was. It didn't take her long to recognize that this man was uncompromisingly male. His eyes held hers reluctantly, as if he, too, was caught in the same powerful trance.

Neither of them moved, and although Shelly was convinced the breathless sensation she felt was a result of the fall, she couldn't seem to breathe properly even now.

"Miss, are you hurt?"

Reluctantly, Shelly looked up to find a security guard standing over her.

"Um . . . I don't think so."

"Sir?"

"I'm fine."

The arms that were holding hers securely began to loosen.

"If we could have you both sit over here for a moment," the guard instructed, pointing at a bench. "We have an ambulance on the way."

"An ambulance? But I told you I'm okay,"

she said.

The guard helped Shelly to her feet. Her legs were shaky and her breathing still uncertain, but otherwise she was unhurt.

"Officer, there's really no need," the man who'd fallen with her protested.

"Mall policy," the guard said. He hooked his thumbs into the wide leather belt and rocked back on his feet. "It's standard procedure to have all accident victims checked immediately."

"If you're worried about a lawsuit —"

"I don't make the rules," the guard interrupted her rescuer. "I just see that they're carried out. Now, if you'd sit over here, the medical team will arrive in a couple of minutes."

"I don't have time to wait," Shelly insisted. "I'm meeting someone." She glanced longingly at the upper level, wondering how she could get word of her delay to Jill. Needless to say, she'd forgotten her cell — could anything else go wrong? It didn't reassure her to notice the number of people clustered by the railing, staring down at her. Her little escapade had attracted quite a bit of attention.

"I've got an appointment, as well," the man said, looking pointedly at his watch.

The security guard ignored their protests.

He removed a small notebook from his shirt pocket and flipped it open. "Your names, please."

"Shelly Hansen."

"Mark Brady."

He wrote down the information and a brief account of how they happened to fall.

"I won't have to go to the hospital, will I?" Shelly demanded.

"That depends," the guard answered.

This whole thing was ridiculous. She was perfectly fine. A little shaken, true, but uninjured. She suddenly realized that she hadn't thanked this man — Mark, was it?

"I'm terribly sorry about all this," she said. "I can't thank you enough for catching me."

"In the future, you might be more careful." Mark glanced at his watch a second time.

"I will be. But if it ever happens again, might I suggest you just let me fall?" This delay was inconvenient, but that wasn't any reason to be quick-tempered. She studied her rescuer and shook her head slightly, wondering why she'd been so impressed. He looked as if he'd stepped off Planet Nerd. Dark blue suit and tie, crisp white shirt, polished loafer-type shoes. This guy was as original as cooked oatmeal. About as personable, too.

If she was giving him the once-over, she discovered he was eyeing her, too. Apparently he was equally unimpressed. Her sweatshirt was a fluorescent orange and her jeans as tight as a second skin. Her ankle-high boots were black, her socks the same shade of orange as the sweatshirt. Her hair cascaded about her shoulders in a layer of dark frothy curls. Mark was scowling in obvious disapproval.

The wide glass doors at the mall entrance opened, and two paramedics hurried inside. Seconds later, when the ambulance arrived, two more medical people entered the building. Shelly was mortified that such a minor accident would result in all this scrutiny.

The first paramedic knelt in front of her while the second concentrated on Mark. Before she completely understood what was happening, her shoe was off and the man was examining her ankle. Mark, too, was being examined, a stethoscope pressed over his heart. He didn't seem to appreciate the procedures any more than she did.

It wasn't until he stood up that she realized how tall he was. Close to six-five, she guessed. A good match for her own five feet ten inches, she thought automatically.

It hit her then. Bull's-eye. Aunt Milly's letter had mentioned her standing beside a tall young man. Mark Brady was tall. Very tall. Taller than just about any man she'd ever met.

Aunt Milly's letter had also said something about Shelly's blue eyes. She'd ignored it at the time, but her eyes weren't blue. They were hazel. Mark had blue eyes, though. The kind of vivid blue eyes women generally found striking . . . Nor could she forget her initial reaction to him. She'd been attracted. Highly attracted. It'd been a long time since a man had interested her this much. Until he stood up, anyway. When she got a good look at him, she'd known immediately that they had nothing in common. She'd bet he didn't own a single article of clothing that wasn't blue, black or tan. Mark Brady was clearly a man without imagination or flair.

On a sudden thought, she glanced worriedly at his left hand. No wedding ring. Closing her eyes, she sagged against the back of the bench and groaned.

"Miss?" The paramedic was studying her closely.

"Excuse me," she said, straightening. She jerked impatiently on Mark's suit jacket. He was involved in a conversation with the ambulance attendant who was interviewing him and didn't turn around.

29

"Excuse me," she said again, louder this time.

"Yes?" Mark turned to face her, frowning impatiently.

Now that she had his attention, she wasn't sure she should continue. "This may seem like an odd question, but, uh . . . are you married?"

He frowned again. "No."

"Oh, no," Shelly moaned and slumped forward. "I was afraid of that."

"I beg your pardon?"

"Do you have a girlfriend? I mean, you're a good-looking guy. There's got to be someone important in your life. Anyone? Please, just think. Surely there's someone?" She knew she was beginning to sound desperate, but she couldn't help it. Aunt Milly's letter was echoing in her mind, and last night's logic had disappeared.

The four paramedics, as well as Mark, were staring at her. "Are you sure you don't want to come to the hospital and talk to a doctor?" one of them asked.

Shelly nodded. "I'm sure." Then before she could stop herself, she blurted out, "What do you do for a living?"

"I'm a CPA," he answered wearily.

"An accountant," she muttered. She should've guessed. He was obviously as staid and conventional as he looked. And as boring. The kind of man who'd probably never even heard of DVDs for entertaining bored house cats. He probably wouldn't be interested in purchasing one, either.

Her aunt Milly *couldn't* have seen Mark and Shelly together in her dream. Not Mark Brady. The two of them were completely ill-suited. A relationship wouldn't last five minutes! Abruptly she reminded herself that she wasn't supposed to be taking Milly's prediction seriously.

"May I go?" she asked the paramedic. "I'm not even bruised."

"Yes, but you'll need to sign here."

Shelly did so without bothering to read the statement. Mark, however, seemed to peruse every sentence. He would, of course.

"Uh, Mark . . ." Shelly hesitated, and Mark glanced in her direction.

"Thank you," she said simply.

"You're welcome."

Still she delayed leaving.

"Is there anything else?"

She didn't know quite how to say this, but she felt the need too strongly to ignore it. "Don't take offense — I'm sure you're a really great guy — but I just want you to know I'm not interested in marriage right now."

THREE

Jill was seated at the table, doodling on the paper place mat, when Shelly arrived. "What kept you?" she asked. "I've been here for almost half an hour."

"I — I fell off the escalator."

Jill's eyes widened in alarm. "My goodness, are you all right?"

Shelly nodded sheepishly. "I'm fine."

"Shouldn't you see a doctor?"

"I already have," she said, avoiding eye contact with her friend. "Well, sort of. The security guard called in the paramedics."

"No wonder you're late."

"I would've been, anyway," Shelly admitted as she reached for a menu, although she knew what she was going to order — the same thing she always did.

"This has really got you flustered, hasn't it?"

"It's more than the fall," Shelly explained, lowering the menu. "It's the man who caught me."

Jill arched her eyebrows jokingly. "Aha! I should have guessed there was a man involved."

"You might try to understand how I felt," Shelly said reproachfully. "Especially since I haven't recovered from receiving Aunt Milly's wedding dress yet."

"Don't tell me you're still worried about that first-man-you-meet nonsense."

"Of course not. That would be ridiculous. It's just . . . it's just I can't help feeling there might be *something* to that silly wedding dress."

"Then mail it back."

"I can't," Shelly said, slapping the menu down on the table. "Aunt Milly warned me not to. She didn't use exactly those words, mind you. She said I shouldn't ignore the dress. I mean, how can I? It's like an albatross around my neck."

"I still think you're overreacting."

"That's the crazy part. I *know* I am, but I can't seem to stop myself. I grew up hearing the legend of that wedding dress, and now it's in my possession. I've got a piece of family history hanging in the back of my closet. What if my mother hears about this?" She shuddered at the thought.

"So you hung the dress in your closet."

"I tried keeping it under my bed, but I couldn't sleep, so I finally got up and stuck it in the closet." She closed the menu and set it aside. "That bothered me, too. I tossed and turned half the night, then I remembered Aunt Milly had done the same thing when the seamstress gave her the dress."

"She put it under her bed?"

Shelly nodded slowly. "I seem to remember hearing that. She'd tried to refuse it, but the old woman insisted Aunt Milly take the gown home with her. By the time she got to her apartment she'd already met my uncle John, although she still didn't know she was going to marry him."

Jill raised a skeptical eyebrow. "Then what? After she put it under her bed and couldn't sleep, I mean?"

"Well, she did the same thing I did," Shelly said. "She shoved it in her closet." Shelly felt as if she was confessing to a crime. "I didn't want the thing staring me in the face so I hung it in the back."

"Naturally." Jill was trying, unsuccessfully, to disguise a smile. Shelly could see how someone else might find her situation humorous, but she personally didn't think any of this was too amusing. Not when it was her life, her future, being tossed around like . . . like some cosmic football. At this rate, she'd be married by nightfall!

"That's not the worst of it," Shelly added. She exhaled slowly, wondering why her heart was still beating so fiercely.

"You mean there's more?"

She nodded. The waitress arrived just then and took their orders, returning quickly with glasses of iced tea. Shelly took a deep breath before she continued. "I literally fell into that man's — Mark Brady's — arms."

"How convenient."

"It's very nice of him to have broken my fall," she said sternly, "but I wish he hadn't."

"Shelly!"

"I mean it." She glanced around to make sure no one was listening, then whispered, "The man's an accountant."

Jill reacted in mock horror, covering her mouth with both hands. "No! An accountant?"

"Think about it. Could you honestly picture me married to an accountant?"

Jill mulled over the question for a moment. "Hmm, a CPA," she repeated slowly. "You still haven't memorized your multiplication tables, have you? You freeze up whenever you have to deal with numbers. No, I guess you're right, I can't see you with an accountant."

Shelly raised both hands, palms up, in a

dramatic gesture. "I rest my case."

Jill reached for some bread, carefully selecting a whole-wheat roll. "Just because you fell into his arms doesn't mean you're going to marry him," she said in a matter-of-fact voice.

"I know that."

"Then what's the problem?"

"I can't make myself *believe* it," Shelly said. "I feel like one tiny pin fighting the force of a giant magnet."

"That's preposterous."

"I know," Shelly agreed readily. "I just wish I hadn't said anything to Mark."

Jill set the roll on her plate with exaggerated care. "You told him about your aunt Milly's wedding dress?"

"Of course not!" Shelly said. "I told him I couldn't marry him."

Jill's mouth dropped open. "You didn't! Did you?"

Shelly nodded. "I don't know what made me say anything so ludicrous. I can't imagine what he must think of me. Not that I plan on seeing him again, of course. Unless —"

"Unless what?"

Their lunches were served. Jill had ordered a hot spinach salad with slices of chicken. Shelly's spinach salad was piled high with shrimp, egg slices and black olives.

"Go on," Jill urged once the waitress had gone. "You don't plan on seeing Mark again unless —"

"Unless it's absolutely unavoidable."

"I take it this means your aunt Milly's first encounter with your uncle John wasn't her last." Jill giggled. "Silly me. Obviously it wasn't."

"No. Even though Aunt Milly didn't want to see him again. My uncle was a wonderful man, don't get me wrong, and he was perfect for Aunt Milly, as it turned out, but they were as different as night and day. Aunt Milly was a college graduate and Uncle John never completed high school."

Shelly sighed wistfully. At one time the story of their romance had been like her own personal fairy tale. But now she didn't find it nearly as enthralling. "He helped Milly fix her car the night it broke down. The very next day she was in court defending a client in a lawsuit —"

"Let me guess," Jill interrupted, "your uncle John was the man suing her client."

Shelly nodded. "Yes, and that was only the beginning. Every time they turned around they were bumping into each other."

"How soon after they met did they get married?"

This was the question Shelly had dreaded most. She closed her eyes and whispered, "Ten days."

"Ten days," Jill echoed with an incredulous look.

"I know. It seems that once they kissed, they both realized there wasn't any use fighting it."

"Did your aunt tell John about the seamstress and the wedding dress?"

Shelly shrugged. "I don't know, but my guess is she didn't . . . at least not at first." She hadn't touched her salad yet and paused to savor a forkful of her favorite seafood. Then she said abruptly, "They eloped without telling anyone."

"Children?" Jill wanted to know.

"Three boys. My mother's cousins."

"What about granddaughters? You'd think your aunt Milly would want to hand the dress down to one of them."

"All three of her sons had boys themselves. I guess you could say I'm the closest she's got to a granddaughter."

"Ten days," Jill repeated. "That's really something."

Forking up another succulent shrimp, Shelly continued her story. "That old Scottish woman knew about the wedding even before the family did. When Aunt Milly and

Uncle John returned from their honeymoon, there was a wedding card from the seamstress waiting for them."

Jill propped her elbows on the table and gazed at Shelly. "Tell me what Mark Brady looks like."

Shelly frowned, trying to form her impressions of him into some kind of reasonably articulate description. He was compelling in ways she didn't quite understand. She sensed that he was principled and headstrong, but what made her so sure of that, Shelly couldn't explain. "He's tall," she began slowly. "And he was wearing a suit."

"How tall?"

"Basketball-player tall. He must be about six-five."

"Brown hair?"

Shelly nodded. "With blue eyes. *Really* blue eyes. I don't think I've ever met a man with eyes that precise color. They seemed to . . ." She hesitated, unsettled by the emotion that stirred within her when she thought about Mark. Although their encounter had been brief, Shelly was left feeling oddly certain that she could trust this man, trust him implicitly. It wasn't a sensation she could remember experiencing with any other man. She didn't like the feeling; it made her uncomfortable. Until Jill had started asking her about Mark, Shelly didn't realize she'd experienced *any* emotion toward him — except for embarrassment, of course.

"Why do you want to know?" she asked.

Jill gave her a knowing grin. "Because if he's as tall as you say, with dark brown hair and deep blue eyes, and he's wearing a suit, he just walked into this restaurant."

"What?" Shelly felt her stomach sink. "Mark's here? Mark Brady?"

"That's not so unusual, is it? This is, after all, the same shopping mall where you, uh, met —" Jill made a show of glancing at her watch "— thirty or so minutes ago."

"He's here." She reminded herself that Jill was right: Mark's choosing to have lunch at Patrick's was just a coincidence. Too bad she couldn't convince her racing heart to believe that.

"He's on the other side of the room," Jill whispered.

"Has he seen me yet?"

"I don't think so."

Without being obvious — or at least Shelly hoped she wasn't being obvious — she turned to look in his direction. At that same instant, Mark happened to look up. Their eyes met. Despite herself, she gasped. Her hands shook and she felt herself break out in a cold sweat.

Mark scowled and quickly looked away.

She couldn't blame him. He seemed surprised to see her there. Unpleasantly surprised.

"Well, is it him?" Jill demanded.

Shelly couldn't find her voice, so she answered with a nod.

"I thought it might be. What are you thinking?"

"That I've lost my appetite." Shelly doubted she'd be able to finish her lunch.

"You want my advice?" Jill asked, grinning broadly. "I don't have a lot of experience with magic wedding dresses, but I recently read a fascinating book on home remedies."

"Sure." At this point Shelly was feeling reckless enough to try just about anything.

"Garlic," Jill said solemnly. "Wear a garlic rope around your neck. Not only does it deter vampires and prevent colds, but it might ward off potential husbands conjured up by a magic wedding dress."

FOUR

Hard though she tried, Shelly had a difficult time ignoring Mark Brady. He sat there, stiff and unapproachable, at the other side of the small restaurant. Just as stiff and unapproachable as she was. Jill wanted to linger over her coffee before returning to her job at the PayRite Pharmacy in the mall, but Shelly was eager to be on her way. The sooner she left, the sooner she could put this bothersome encounter behind her.

"Don't forget Morgan's baby shower on Tuesday night," Jill said as Shelly reached for her purse.

Shelly had completely forgotten about their friend's party, which was understandable given her present state of mind. Most of their college friends were married and several were now having babies. Rather than admit how absentminded she'd suddenly become, Shelly asked, "Do you want to drive over together?"

"Sure," Jill said. "I have to go directly from work so I'll stop off at your place and we can leave from there."

"I'll be ready." She tried to imagine their excitable classmate as a wife and mother. It was Morgan who'd gotten the entire dorm hooked on *Survivor.* Before anyone could figure out how it had occurred, all the girls were obsessed with the participants and their lives. It became as important as mealtimes to learn who'd been voted off and who'd won that week's challenges.

For no particular reason, Shelly thought of Aunt Milly's wedding dress — which seemed to have become her own private challenge. Sighing, she dropped her share of the bill and a tip on the table. "I'll see you Tuesday, then."

"Right. And, Shelly, don't look so worried. No enchanted wedding dress is going to interfere with your life — unless you allow it to."

Easy for Jill to say, since it wasn't *her* life and *her* great-aunt's wedding dress. Nevertheless, her advice was sound. Aunt Milly might have had some fanciful dream about Shelly's marrying a tall man with blue eyes, but that didn't mean it was going to happen, especially when Shelly was so determined that it wouldn't.

"You're absolutely right," she said emphatically. "I know I keep saying that, but . . . well, I seem to need reminding. So, thanks. Again." With a final wave, she wandered out of the restaurant, barely noticing the colorful shop windows as she passed them. As Jill had pointed out, Aunt Milly meant well, but the letter and the wedding dress shouldn't be taken too seriously.

Shelly knew exactly what kind of man she'd fall in love with, and he wouldn't bear any resemblance to Mark Brady. He'd be unconventional, and fervent about life, and as passionate as she was herself. Naturally, he'd appreciate her work and take pride in his own. He'd be a free spirit, like her. She'd prefer a man with gumption, too — someone who possessed initiative. It'd be nice if he was a little better at organizational skills than she was, but that wasn't a requirement.

With marriage so prominent in her mind, Shelly found herself standing in front of a jeweler's display window, studying a large assortment of wedding bands. She noticed one ring that stood out from the rest: three small rows of diamond chips, bracketed on each side by a thin band of gold. The ring was striking in its simplicity, its uncontrived beauty.

For the longest moment Shelly stared at the rings as she wove whimsical dreams around the happy bride and the tall groom. *Tall groom.* Her thoughts came to a skidding halt.

What on earth had come over her? She didn't know, but whatever it was, she didn't like it. Self-consciously she glanced around, fearful that someone was watching her. Well, a very specific someone, to be honest. Someone who definitely shouldn't see her gazing with open longing at a collection of absurdly high-priced wedding rings. Mark Brady.

With a sense of urgency, Shelly hurried toward the mall exit. It was all she could do to keep from breaking into a run. No matter how fast she walked, however, she couldn't shake the feeling that *he* was there, watching her. Twice she whirled around, convinced she'd see Mark Brady strolling behind her, sneering and making contemptuous remarks.

He wasn't there.

With profound relief, she arrived at the parking lot and located her car. She finally felt herself relax as she neared her apartment building. Once she'd parked her car, Shelly stopped in the lobby to collect her mail. As soon as she opened the small box,

Mrs. Livingston's head poked out her door.

"Good afternoon, Shelly," she chirped, smiling at her expectantly.

It took Shelly a moment to realize that Mrs. L. must have been waiting to hear about the contents of her package.

"It's a lovely day," Shelly said conversationally, sorting through her mail. Two bills, a flyer and something from the Internal Revenue Service. The way her luck had been going, it was probably an audit notice. A quick inspection revealed exactly that. She closed her eyes and groaned inwardly.

"A lovely day indeed," Mrs. Livingston echoed cheerfully.

Muttering under her breath, Shelly stuffed the IRS notice back inside the envelope. When she looked up, she saw that the older woman was now standing in the hallway.

"I suppose you're wondering about the package," Shelly said resignedly, tucking her mail inside her purse. "It was a gift from my aunt Milly."

"Something from the past, I guess?" Mrs. Livingston asked.

"Why . . . yes. How'd you know?"

"I'd take whatever it is very, very seriously if I were you," Mrs. Livingston continued in a solemn voice. "Wizard wouldn't go anywhere near that box. Think what you want,

46

but my cat's always had a sixth sense when it comes to this sort of thing."

"It's a dress, Mrs. L.," Shelly explained, hiding behind a false smile. "How am I supposed to take a dress seriously?" It was exactly what she'd vowed *not* to do.

Mrs. Livingston opened her apartment door and scooped the large black-and-white cat into her arms. "That I wouldn't know," she returned, her eyes narrowed. "All I can tell you is that Wizard felt skittish around that package. You don't suppose there's . . . magic in it, do you?"

Somehow Shelly managed a reply, although she felt certain it was unintelligible. Taking the stairs two at a time, she dashed into her apartment, leaning breathlessly against the door. Even Mrs. Livingston's cat knew there was something strange about Aunt Milly's wedding dress!

When Jill arrived late Tuesday afternoon, Shelly was ready and waiting for her, brightly wrapped baby gift in hand. She was eager to get out and socialize — eager to get out, period. Anything to escape another phone call from her mother, who'd recently heard from Aunt Milly. Now Faith Hansen was calling daily for updates on the romantic prospects in her daughter's life.

"Well?" Jill demanded as she entered the apartment. "Are you going to show it to me?"

"Show what to you?"

Jill gave her a look that seemed to question her intelligence. "The wedding dress, of course."

For several hours Shelly had succeeded in putting the dress out of her mind. "No," she said forcefully. "I want to forget about the whole thing."

"Met any tall blue-eyed men lately?" Jill couldn't resist asking.

"None," Shelly answered shortly. Checking her watch, she noted that they were early but suggested they leave, anyway. "Shall we go?"

"We've got lots of time," Jill countered, moving toward Shelly's bedroom. "Come on, it isn't going to hurt to let me look at the dress."

"Oh, all right," Shelly conceded ungraciously. Leading the way, she opened the closet door and reached into the back of the closet.

She brought out the lace-and-satin gown, holding it up for Jill's inspection. She'd hardly looked at the dress the day she'd received it, and now she was almost shocked by how beautiful it actually was.

The laughter drained from Jill's dark brown eyes as she stared at the gown. "Oh, Shelly, it's . . . lovely." She gently touched the Elizabethan sleeve and ran her finger along the delicate layer of pearls that decorated the cuff. The high neckline was also trimmed with an intricate design of pearls. "I don't know what I expected," Jill said in an awed whisper, "but certainly nothing as beautiful as this."

Shelly nodded wordlessly. The dress was far more exquisite than she'd realized. Her heart swelled with sudden emotion, and to her dismay, tears filled her eyes as she thought about the old Scottish woman who had so lovingly constructed the gown. Each pearl had been sewn into place by hand. She thought of her aunt Milly, as tall and statuesque as Shelly herself, wearing the dress. Then she recalled her uncle John, such a determined man, so wise and sensible. Shelly thought fondly of those two, who'd been so completely different, yet had loved each other so well. . . .

For a moment neither she nor Jill spoke. "Have you tried it on?" Jill finally asked.

Shelly shook her head adamantly, not wanting her friend to know how emotional she'd become. "Heavens, no, but you can if you want."

"I don't think I could resist if I were you," Jill whispered, obviously affected by the dress, too. "Just seeing it . . . makes me wish I was a bride myself."

"There's always Ralph," Shelly teased. Jill had been dating Ralph, a computer programmer, for several months, but Shelly couldn't understand what her friend saw in him.

Jill threw her an irritated look. "The dress is for you, not me."

"But I don't want it," Shelly insisted, though she was no longer sure what she felt. Not since she'd really examined the dress and allowed herself to remember the wonder of John and Milly's romance.

"You're sure you don't mind?" Jill asked, slipping off her shoes. "I mean, if you'd rather I didn't try it on, I'll understand."

"No, feel free." Shelly strove for a flippant air. "As far as I'm concerned, the dress is nothing but bad luck. It arrived on Friday the thirteenth. The next day I had that minor accident on the mall escalator. Now I'm being audited by the IRS."

It was as if Jill didn't hear. "I doubt it'll fit," she said as she cautiously removed the gown from the padded hanger. "I'm a good five inches shorter than you and heavier on top."

"Maybe the dress was meant for you in the first place," Shelly ventured. Perhaps Aunt Milly had been confused and it was Jill she'd viewed in her dream. After all, Milly's eyes weren't what they used to be. . . .

"Does your mother know?" Jill asked as she stepped into the dress. She raised it over her hips and turned around to let Shelly fasten the buttons that ran down the back.

"That's another thing," Shelly moaned. "Mom's been calling me every day since I got the dress, wanting to know if I've met anyone special yet."

"What did you tell her?" Jill asked, looking at Shelly over her shoulder.

"What's there to tell?" she asked irritably.

"Well, you might have mentioned Mark."

"Mark," Shelly repeated. She shrugged elaborately. "I haven't given him a thought in days." Not strictly true, but she'd been *trying* not to think about him. Even if he was interested in her — and he'd made very clear that he wasn't — she couldn't imagine two more ill-suited people. "I haven't seen him since Saturday and I doubt I'll ever see him again."

"You're sure of that?"

"Positive."

"Well, what do you think?" Jill asked next, pirouetting slowly in front of her. "My hair's a mess and I've got hardly any makeup on, but . . ."

Shelly studied her friend and sighed audibly. Never had she seen Jill look lovelier. It was as if the dress had been made for her. "Absolutely enchanting. It fits like a dream."

"I feel like I *am* dreaming," Jill admitted softly. "Here," she said, turning around, "undo me before I start longing for a husband and 2.5 children."

"Don't forget the house with the white picket fence," Shelly teased, unfastening the buttons.

Jill slipped out of the dress. "Your turn," she said as she laid it carefully across the bed. "If it fits me, then it can't possibly fit you. You've got the perfect excuse to send it back to your aunt Milly."

"I . . . don't know." Shelly bit her lip. She felt an inexplicable urge to keep the dress, and at the same time she would've willingly returned it to her aunt. Even while she hesitated, Shelly found herself undressing. She couldn't explain her sudden eagerness to try on the wedding gown any more than she could fathom its growing emotional appeal.

The dress slid easily over her hips. She turned around so Jill could secure the back, then glanced at the mirror, expecting to find the skirt miles too short. It would have to be in order to fit Jill as perfectly as it had.

"Shelly," Jill whispered, then cupped her hand over her mouth. "My goodness . . . you look beautiful . . . really beautiful."

That was what Shelly had felt the instant she'd seen her friend in the dress. "Something's wrong," she said once she found her voice. "Something's very wrong."

"No," Jill countered, "it's very right. It's as if the dress was made for you."

"Then answer me this," Shelly whispered. "How is it possible for the same dress to fit two women who wear totally different sizes?"

FIVE

Shelly struggled to open the door of the Internal Revenue office, her arms weighed down with a huge box stuffed full of receipts and records for the audit. By bracing the box against the wall with her knee, she freed one hand to open the door. For the first time ever, she'd completed her tax return early — all by herself, too — and *this* was her reward. She grumbled righteously and bit her lip, more in anxiety than annoyance.

She'd just managed to grasp the door handle, when the door unexpectedly opened and she staggered into the room, nearly colliding with an end table. She did a quick pirouette, convinced she'd ruined a new pair of panty hose. With a heartfelt sigh, she set her box of records on the floor and sank into the first available chair, neatly arranging her unaccustomed skirt around her knees. Only then did she bother to look around. There was one other person in the large reception area.

Shelly's heart did a nosedive, landing in the pit of her stomach. The man who'd opened the door for her, the man sitting in this very waiting room, was none other than Mark Brady — the man she'd hoped to avoid for the rest of her natural life. She gave an involuntary gasp.

Mark was leafing through the dog-eared pages of a magazine when he happened to glance her way. The automatic smile faded from his face, and his eyes narrowed as if he strongly suspected Shelly had purposely arranged this meeting.

"What are you doing here?" Shelly demanded.

"I might ask you the same thing."

"I didn't follow you here, if that's what you're implying!"

"Listen, Ms. . . . Hansen, I really couldn't care less." With that he returned to his magazine, but he raised his head again a moment later. "*You're* the person who blurted out to everyone within hearing distance that you weren't marrying me. As if I'd even asked! As if I even *knew* you!"

Shelly felt the heat rising up her neck and offered the first excuse she could think of. "I . . . was distraught."

"Obviously," he muttered from behind his

magazine.

A few minutes of strained silence passed. Shelly shifted uncomfortably in her chair, checking her watch approximately every ten seconds. She was early for her appointment, but if this was where promptness got you, she'd prefer to be late.

"All right, I apologize," Shelly said when she couldn't tolerate the silence any longer. "What I said was ridiculous and . . . and out of turn —"

"Out of turn," Mark echoed, throwing the magazine down on the table. "I repeat — I don't even know you."

"I realize that."

He inhaled deeply, which drew her attention to his broad, muscular chest. She saw that he was as meticulously dressed as he'd been at their first encounter. His dark suit and silk tie, however conventional, added a touch of sophistication to his natural good looks.

"If there's anyone to blame for this it's Aunt Milly," Shelly said, more to herself than him.

"Aunt Milly?" Mark repeated, sounding unsure. He eyed her warily.

She'd said this much; she might as well launch into the whole ludicrous tale.

"Actually, it has more to do with the wedding dress than with my aunt Milly, although by now the two of them are inseparable in my mind. I don't usually dabble in this sort of thing, but I'm beginning to think there might be something supernatural about that silly dress, after all."

"Supernatural?"

"Magic, if you prefer."

"Magic in a wedding dress?" Mark gazed hopefully at the door that led to the inner offices of Internal Revenue, as though he was anxious to be called away.

"It's unbelievable, but the dress fits both Jill and me, which is virtually impossible. You saw Jill — she's the friend I was having lunch with last Saturday. I know we were halfway across the room from you, but you couldn't help noticing how much shorter she is than I am. We're completely different sizes."

Mark hurriedly reached for the magazine as if he wanted to shut her out before she said anything else.

"I know it seems crazy. I don't like this any better than you do, but I'm afraid you're the one Aunt Milly mentioned in her letter." Well, it was only fair to tell him that.

Mark glanced in her direction again, blue eyes suspicious. "Your aunt Milly mentioned me in a letter?"

"Not by name — but she said she had a clear vision of me in the wedding dress and I was standing with a tall man. She also referred to blue eyes. You're tall and you have blue eyes and the legend says I'm going to marry the first man I meet after receiving the dress."

"And I just happened to be that man?"

"Yes," Shelly cried. "*Now* do you understand why I was so disturbed when we met?"

"Not entirely," Mark said after a moment.

Shelly sighed loudly. How obtuse could the man be? "You're tall, aren't you? And you have blue eyes."

He flipped intently through the magazine, not looking at her as he spoke. "I really don't care what the letter said, nor am I concerned about this wedding dress you keep bringing up."

"Of course you don't care," Shelly said indignantly. "Why should you? It must all seem quite absurd to you. And I'm aware that I'm overreacting, but I do have a tendency to get emotional. If it helps any, I want you to know I'm happy with my life just the way it is. I don't want to get married — to anyone." When she'd finished, she drew in a deep breath and began leafing idly through a magazine, doing her utmost to ignore him.

Silence returned. Silences had always bothered Shelly. It was as if she felt personally responsible for filling them. "If you want something to be grateful about, you can thank your lucky stars I didn't mention you to my mother."

"Your mother," Mark repeated. "Does she know about Aunt Milly sending you this . . . dress?"

"Of course she does," Shelly answered, closing the magazine. "She's phoned me every day since she heard, because she thinks I'm going to meet that special someone any minute."

"And you didn't say anything about me?"

"How could I? The instant I do that, she'll be calling the caterers."

"I see." The edges of his mouth lifted as though he was beginning to find the situation amusing. "She believes in the power of this dress, too?"

"Unfortunately, yes. You have to understand where my mother stands on the issue of marriage," Shelly continued, undaunted.

"I'm not sure I want to," Mark muttered under his breath.

Shelly disregarded his comment. "By age twenty-eight — my age now, coincidentally — Mom had been married for eight years and already had three children. She's convinced I'm letting the best years of my life slip away. There's nothing I can say to make her believe differently."

"Then I'll add my gratitude that you didn't mention me."

Mollified, Shelly nodded, then glanced at her watch. Her meeting was in ten minutes and she was nervous, since this was the first time she'd done her own taxes. She should have known there'd be a problem.

"I take it you're here for an audit?" Mark asked.

She nodded again, studying her tax return, sure she'd be in jail by nightfall without even understanding what she'd done wrong.

"Relax."

"How can I?"

"Have you knowingly hidden something from the government? Lied about the income you received, or claimed expenditures you've never made?"

"Oh, no!"

"Then you don't have anything to worry about."

"I don't?" Shelly stared at him, envying his confidence. She'd been restless for days, worrying about this meeting. If it wasn't the wedding dress giving her nightmares, it was the audit.

"Don't volunteer any information unless

they ask for it."

"All right."

"Did you prepare your own tax return?"

"Well, yes. It didn't seem that complicated, and well, this sounds silly but Jill bet me I couldn't do it. So I did. Back in February. You see, numbers tend to confuse me and I decided to accept the challenge, and . . ." She realized she was chattering, something she did when she was nervous. Forcing herself to stay quiet, she scanned her return for the hundredth time, wondering what she could have possibly done wrong.

"Do you want me to look it over for you?"

Shelly was surprised by his generosity. "If you wouldn't mind. Are you being audited yourself?"

Mark smiled and shook his head. "A client of mine is."

"Oh."

He crossed the room and sat next to her. When Shelly handed him her tax return, he quickly ran down the row of figures, then asked her several questions.

"I've got everything right here," she assured him, gesturing toward the carton she'd lugged in with her. "I really am careful about saving everything I should."

Mark gestured at the large cardboard box.

61

"This is all for one year?"

"No," she admitted sheepishly. "I brought along everything I had for the past six years. I mean, it made sense at the time."

"That really wasn't necessary."

"I'd rather be safe than sorry," Shelly said with a shrug. She watched Mark as he scrutinized her return. At such close range, she saw that his eyes were even bluer than she'd thought. *Blue as the sky on a bright July afternoon . . .* Her heart felt heavy in her chest, and hard as she tried, she couldn't keep herself from staring.

Mark handed back her return. "Everything looks fine. I don't think you'll have a problem."

It was astonishing how relieved she felt at hearing that. No, at hearing that from *him*. Mark smiled at her and Shelly found herself responding readily with a smile of her own. The fluttery sensation returned to her stomach. She knew her eyes were wide and questioning and although she tried to look away, she couldn't do it.

Surprise mingled with gentleness on his face, as if he were seeing her for the first time, really seeing her. He liked what he saw — Shelly could read that in his eyes. Slowly his gaze traveled over her features, and she felt her pulse speed up. The letter she'd received from Aunt Milly flitted through her mind, but instead of dismissing the memory, she wondered, *Could there really be something to all this?*

Mark was the one to break eye contact. He stood abruptly and hurried back to his seat. "I don't think you have to worry."

"Yes, you told me."

"I mean about your aunt Milly's wedding dress."

"I don't have to worry?" Shelly repeated. She wasn't sure she understood.

"Not with me, at any rate."

"I don't quite follow. . . ." If he was even half-aware of the way her heart was clamoring as they gazed into each other's eyes, he wouldn't be nearly as confident.

"I'm engaged."

"Engaged?" Shelly felt as though someone had slugged her in the stomach. Her first reaction was anger. "You couldn't have mentioned this sooner?" she snapped.

"It's not official yet. Janice hasn't picked out a diamond. Nor have we discussed our plans with her family."

The irritation faded, swallowed by an overwhelming sense of relief. "Engaged," she murmured, reminding herself that she really had no interest in marriage. And this proved there was no such thing as a "magic" wedding dress. If Mark was involved with Janice, he wouldn't be free to marry her. It was that simple. Shelly leaped to her feet and started to pace.

"Are you all right?" Mark asked. "You're looking pale."

She nodded and pressed her hands to her cheeks, which suddenly felt hot. "I'm so relieved," she whispered hoarsely. "You have no idea how relieved I am. You're engaged . . . My goodness, I feel like I've got a new lease on life."

"As I explained," Mark said, frowning, "it isn't official yet."

"That's okay. You're committed to someone else and that's all that matters. However —" she forced a smile "— you might have said something sooner and saved me all this anxiety."

"You did ask that day at the mall, but I was more concerned with avoiding a scene than revealing the personal details of my life."

"I'm sorry about that."

"No problem."

Shelly settled back in the chair and crossed her legs, hoping to strike a relaxed pose. She even managed to skim a couple of magazines, although she barely knew what she was reading.

Finally, the receptionist opened the door and called her name. Eager to get this over with, Shelly stood, picking up the large box she'd brought with her. She paused on her way out of the reception area and turned to Mark. "I wish you and Janice every happiness," she said formally.

"Thank you," he answered, then grinned. "Same to you and whatever, uh, lucky guy the wedding dress finds you."

Six

She should be happy, Shelly told herself early the following morning. Not only had she survived the audit — in fact she'd come away with an unexpected refund — but she'd learned that Mark was practically engaged.

Yes, she should be dancing in the streets, singing in the aisles . . . Instead she'd been struggling with a strange melancholy ever since their last encounter. She seemed to have lost her usual vitality, her sense of fun.

Now it was Saturday, and for once she had no looming deadlines, no appointments, no pressing errands. Remembering the exhilaration and solace she'd felt when she recorded an ocean storm sequence recently, Shelly decided to see if she could recapture some of those feelings. She headed over to Long Beach, a resort town on the Washington coastline. The sky was clear and almost cloudless; the sun was bright and pleasantly warm — a perfect spring day. Once she drove onto the freeway, the miles sped past and two hours later she was standing on the sandy beach with the breeze riffling her long hair.

She walked around for a while, enjoying the sights and sounds — the chirping of the sea gulls, the salty spray of the Pacific Ocean and the scent of wind and sea. She was satisfied with her beach DVD and started to work out plans for a whole series — the ocean in different seasons, different moods. That would be something special, she thought, something unique.

She wandered down the beach, kicking at the sand with the toes of her running shoes. Tucking her fingertips in the pockets of her jeans, she breathed in the vivid freshness around her. After an hour or so, she made her way back to the concession stands, where she bought a hot dog and a cold drink.

Then, just because it looked like fun, she rented a moped.

She sped along the shore, thrilled with the sensation of freedom, reveling in the solitude and the roar of pounding surf.

The wind tossed her hair about her face until it was a confusion of curls. Shelly laughed aloud and listened as the galloping breeze carried off the sound.

Her motorized bike rushed forward, spitting sand in its wake. She felt reckless with exhilaration, as though there was nothing she couldn't do. It was that kind of afternoon. That kind of day.

When she least expected it, someone else on a moped raced past her. Shelly hadn't encountered anyone during her ride and this person took her by surprise. She glanced quickly over her shoulder, astonished by how far she'd traveled. The only other person she could see was the one who'd passed her.

To her surprise, the rider did an abrupt turnaround and headed back in her direction. With the sun in her eyes and the wind pelting her, Shelly slowed to a crawl and shaded her eyes with one hand.

It wasn't until he was nearly beside her that Shelly recognized the other rider.

Mark Brady.

She was so shocked that she allowed the engine to die, her feet dropping to the sand to maintain her balance. Mark appeared equally shocked. He braked abruptly.

"Shelly?" He seemed not to believe it was her.

Shelly shook her head and blinked a couple of times just to make sure she wasn't fantasizing. She certainly hadn't expected to encounter Mark Brady on a beach two hours out of Seattle. Mr. Conservative riding a moped! This time, though, he wasn't wearing a dark suit. He didn't have his briefcase with him, either. And he looked even handsomer than usual in worn jeans and a University of Washington sweatshirt.

"Mark?" She couldn't prevent the astonishment from creeping into her voice.

"What are you doing here?"

She heard the hostility in his tone and answered him coolly. "The same thing as you, apparently." She pushed the hair from her face, and the wind promptly blew it back.

Mark's blue eyes narrowed suspiciously. "You didn't happen to follow me, did you?"

"Follow you?" she repeated indignantly. She'd rarely been more insulted. "Follow you!" she said again, starting her moped and revving the engine. "May I remind you that I was on the beach first? If anyone was doing any following, it was *you* following me." She was breathless by the time she finished. "In fact, you're the last person I'd follow anywhere!"

Mark scowled at her. "The feeling's mutual. I'm not in the mood for another story about your aunt Martha's damn wedding dress, either."

Shelly felt an unexpected flash of pain. "I was having a perfectly wonderful afternoon until you arrived," she said stiffly.

"I was having a good time myself," he muttered.

"Then I suggest we go our separate ways and forget we ever met."

Mark looked as if he was about to say something else, but Shelly was in no frame of mind to listen. She twisted the accelerator on the handlebar of her moped and took off down the beach. Although she knew she was being unreasonable, she was furious. Furious at the surge of joy she'd felt when she recognized him. Furious at Mark, because he didn't seem even a little pleased to see her. She bit her lower lip, remembering the comment he'd made about not wanting to hear any more about her "damn wedding dress." Now, that was just rude, she told herself righteously. She could *never* be interested in a man who was not only conventional but rude.

Squinting, Shelly hunched her shoulders against the wind, in a hurry now to return to the boardwalk. She hadn't meant to go nearly this far.

The wet, compact sand made for smooth, fast riding and Shelly stayed close to the water's edge in an effort to outdistance Mark. Not that he was likely to chase her, but she wanted to avoid any possibility of another embarrassing encounter.

Then it happened.

A large wave came in, sneaking its way up the sand, creating a thin, glistening sheen. Shelly hardly noticed as her front tire ripped through the water, spraying it out on both sides. Then the moped's front wheel dipped precariously. One minute she was sailing down the beach at breakneck speed and the next she was cartwheeling over her handlebars.

She landed heavily in a patch of wet sand, too paralyzed with shock to know if she was hurt or not.

Before she could move, Mark was crouching at her side. "Shelly? Are you all right?"

"I . . . don't know." Carefully she flexed one arm and then the other. Sitting up, she tested each leg and didn't feel pain there, either. Apparently she'd survived the experience unscathed.

"You crazy fool!" he yelled, leaping to his feet. "What are you trying to do, kill yourself?"

"Ah . . ." It was painful to breathe, otherwise she would've answered him.

"Can you imagine what I thought when I

saw you flying through the air like that?"

"Good riddance?" she suggested.

Mark closed his eyes and shook his head. "I'm in no mood for your jokes. Here, let me help you up." He moved behind her, sliding his arms around her waist and gently raising her.

"I'm fine," she protested the instant his arms surrounded her. The blood rushed to her head, but Shelly didn't know if that was because of her tumble or because Mark was holding her. Even when she was on her feet, he didn't release her.

"Are you sure you're not hurt?"

Shelly nodded, not trusting her voice. "I'm less confident about the moped, though." Her bike seemed to be in worse shape than she was.

"It doesn't look good to me, either," Mark said. He finally dropped his arms and retrieved the moped, which was lying on its side, the waves lapping over it. There were regular hissing sounds as the cold water splashed against the heated muffler. Steam rose from the engine.

Mark did his best to start the bike, but to no avail. "I'm afraid it's hopelessly wet. It won't start now until it's had a chance to dry. A mechanic should check it over to be sure nothing's wrong."

Shelly agreed. There was no help for it; she was going to have to walk the bike back to the rental shop. No small feat when she considered she was about three miles down the beach.

"Thank you very much for stopping," she said a bit primly. "But as you can see I'm not hurt. . . ."

"What do you think you're doing?" Mark asked as she began pushing the moped. It made for slow progress; the bulky machine was far more difficult to transport under her own power than she'd expected. At this rate, she'd be lucky to return it by nightfall.

"I'm taking the bike back to the place where I rented it."

"That's ridiculous."

"Do you have any better ideas?" she asked in a reasonable tone of voice. "I don't understand what you're doing here in the first place," she said, sounding far calmer than she felt. "You should be with Janet."

"Who?" he demanded. He tried to take the moped away from her and push it himself, but she wouldn't let go.

"The woman you're going to marry. Remember?"

"Her name is Janice and as I said before, the engagement's unofficial."

"That doesn't answer my question. You

should be with her on a beautiful spring day like this."

Mark frowned. "Janice couldn't get away. She had an important meeting with a client — she's a lawyer. Listen, quit being so stubborn, I'm stronger than you. Let me push the bike."

Shelly hesitated; his offer was tempting. She hadn't gone more than a few feet and already her side ached. She pressed one hand against her hip and straightened, her decision made. "Thanks, but no thanks," she answered flatly. "By the way, it's Aunt Milly who sent me the wedding dress, not Aunt Martha, so if we're going to get names straight, let's start there."

Mark rolled his eyes skyward, as though he'd reached the end of his limited patience. "Fine, I'll apologize for what I said back there. I didn't mean to insult you."

"I didn't follow you," she said.

"I know, but I didn't follow you, either."

Shelly nodded, deciding she believed him.

"Then how do you explain that we've inadvertently bumped into each other twice in the last week?" Mark asked. "The odds of that happening have got to be phenomenal."

"I know it sounds crazy, but . . . I'm afraid it's the dress," Shelly mumbled.

"The wedding dress?" Mark repeated.

"I'm really embarrassed about all this. I'm not sure I believe any of it myself. And I do apologize, especially since there's been an apparent mix-up. . . ."

"Why's that?" Mark asked.

"Well . . . because you're involved with Janice. I'm sure the two of you are a perfect match and you'll have a marvelous life together."

"What makes you assume that?"

His question caught her off guard. "Well, because . . . didn't you just tell me you're about to become officially engaged?"

"Yes," he muttered.

Although she was reluctant to admit it, Shelly found pushing the moped extremely taxing, so she stopped to rest for a moment. "Listen," she said a little breathlessly, "there's no need for you to walk with me. Why don't you just go on ahead?"

"There most definitely is a need," Mark answered sharply. He didn't seem too pleased with her suggestion. "I'm not going to desert you now."

"Oh, Mark, honestly, you don't have to be such a gentleman."

"You don't like gentlemen?"

"Of course I do — but it's one of the reasons you and I would never get along for

75

any length of time. You're very sweet, don't get me wrong, but I don't need anyone to rescue me."

"Forgive me for saying so, but you *do* appear to need rescuing." The look he gave her implied that he was referring to more than the moped.

"I was the one foolish enough to get the engine wet," she said brightly, ignoring his comment. "So I should be the one to deal with the consequences."

Mark waited a moment, as if debating whether to continue arguing. "Fine, if that's the way you feel," he said finally, straddling his moped and starting the engine, which roared to life with sickening ease. "I hope you don't tire out too quickly."

"I'll be okay," she said, hardly able to believe he was actually going to abandon her.

"I hope you're right about that," he said, revving the engine.

"You . . . you could let someone know," she ventured. Maybe the rental agency would send someone out with a truck to find her.

"I'll see what I can do," he agreed, then grinning broadly, took off at top speed down the beach.

Although she'd made the suggestion that

he go on without her, Shelly had assumed he wouldn't take it seriously. She'd said it more for the sake of dignity, of preserving her pride. She'd been enjoying his company, enjoying the banter between them.

As he vanished into the distance, Shelly squared her shoulders, determined to manage on her own — particularly since she didn't have any choice. She'd been dragging her moped along for perhaps ten minutes when she noticed another moped racing toward her. It didn't take her long to identify the rider, with his lithe, muscular build, as Mark. She picked up her pace, unreasonably pleased that he'd decided to return. He slowed as he approached her.

"Still eager to be rid of me?"

"No," she admitted, smiling half in relief, half in pleasure. "Can't you tell when a woman means something and when she's just being polite?"

"I guess not." He smiled back, apparently in a jovial mood. "Rest," he said, parking his own moped and taking hers. "A truck will be along any minute."

Shelly sank gratefully down on the lush sand. Mark lowered himself onto the beach beside her. She plucked several blades of grass and began weaving them industriously together. That way, she wouldn't have to look at him.

"Are you always this stubborn?" he asked.

"Yes," she said quietly, giving him a shy smile. Shelly couldn't remember being shy in her life. But something about Mark made her feel shaky inside, and oddly weak. An unfamiliar sensation, but she dared not analyze it, dared not examine it too closely. She turned away from him and closed her eyes, trying to picture Janice, the woman he was going to marry. Despite her usually creative imagination, Shelly couldn't seem to visualize her.

"Shelly, what's wrong?"

"Wrong?"

"It's not like you to be so quiet."

She grinned. They were barely more than acquaintances, and he already knew her. "Nothing."

"I think there must be." His finger against the side of her face guided her eyes toward him. Their lips were so close. Shelly's breath seemed to be caught in her throat as she stared helplessly into the bluest eyes she'd ever seen. . . .

His forehead touched hers, then he angled his face, brushing her cheek. Shelly knew she should break away, but she couldn't make herself do it. Gently, deliberately, he pressed his mouth to hers, his lips warm and moist.

Shelly moaned at the shock of sensation. Her eyes drifted shut as his mouth moved hungrily over hers, and soon their arms were wrapped tightly around each other, their bodies straining close.

The sound of the approaching truck intruded into their private world and broke them apart. Mark's eyes met hers, then he scowled and glanced away. But Shelly didn't know whether he was angry with her or with himself. Probably her.

SEVEN

"Hey," Shelly said reassuringly, "don't look so concerned. It was just an ordinary, run-of-the-mill kiss." She stood and brushed the wet sand from her jeans. "Besides, it didn't mean anything."

Mark's scowl darkened. "Didn't mean anything?" he echoed.

"Of course it didn't! I mean, we were both wondering what it would be like, don't you think? Good grief, we seem to be running into each other every other day and it's only logical that we'd want to, you know, experiment."

"In other words, you think the kiss was just a means of satisfying our mutual curiosity?"

"Sure. All this nonsense about the wedding dress overcame our common sense, and we succumbed to temptation." Thank goodness Mark seemed to understand her rambling. Shelly's knees were shaking. It was a wonder she could still stand upright. Although she'd tried to minimize the effects of his kiss, it left her feeling as though she'd never been kissed before. Her entire body had been overwhelmed by a feeling of *rightness*. Now all she felt was the crushing weight of confusion. She shouldn't be feeling any of these things for Mark. A CPA! An almost-engaged CPA, to boot.

"And was your curiosity satisfied?" he asked. His blue eyes probed.

"Uh . . . yes. And yours?"

"Yes," he muttered, but he was frowning again.

The kid from the rental agency leaped out of the truck and loaded Shelly's moped into the back. "You're not supposed to get the engine wet," he scolded. "It's in the rental agreement. You'll have to pay a fine."

Shelly nodded. She didn't have an excuse; she doubted the agency would accept her trying to escape Mark as a legitimate reason for damaging one of their vehicles.

Mark drove his moped, while Shelly got into the pickup's cab and rode silently down the long stretch of beach.

Shelly went to the office to deal with her fine and was surprised to find Mark waiting for her when she'd finished. "You hungry?" he asked in an offhand invitation.

"Uh . . ." She would've thought he'd be anxious to see the last of her.

"Good," he said immediately, not giving her a chance to reply. He grasped her elbow firmly as he led her to a nearby fish-and-chips stand. Shelly couldn't recall any other time a man had taken her elbow. Her first reaction was to object to what she considered an outdated gesture but she was surprised to find it oddly comforting, even pleasant.

They ordered their fish and chips, then carried the small baskets to a picnic table.

"I should've paid for my own," she said once they were seated, feeling vaguely guilty that he'd paid for both meals. Janice might be the jealous type, and Shelly didn't want her to hear about this.

His eyes met hers, steady and direct. "When I ask you to join me, I pick up the bill."

Any argument she had vanished before it reached her lips.

After that, Shelly concentrated on her fish and chips, which were fresh and absolutely delicious. Mark seemed equally preoccupied with his meal.

"What brought you to the beach today?" Shelly asked, finishing the last few French fries in her basket. Perhaps if they could determine what had brought them both to a lonely stretch of beach two hours from Seattle, they might be able to figure out how they'd happened upon each other once more.

"I have a beach house here. After tax time I generally try to get away for a few days. I like to come down here and relax."

"I had no idea." She found it inordinately important that he understand she hadn't somehow managed to stalk him across the state. Their meeting was pure coincidence . . . again.

"Don't worry about it, Shelly. You couldn't possibly have known about the beach house or that I intended to be here today. I didn't know it myself until this morning."

Shelly suddenly wished Mark hadn't kissed her. Everything was becoming far too complicated.

"You're very talented," he told her out of the blue. "I bought one of your DVDs the other day."

"How'd you know what I do?" Shelly felt flustered by his praise; she was at a complete loss to understand why it meant so much to her.

"I saw it on the income tax form and I was curious about your work."

"Curiosity seems to have gotten us both

into trouble," she said.

Mark grinned, a shameless, irresistible grin. The kind of grin that makes a woman forget all sorts of things. Like the fact that he was practically engaged. And that he was a tall, blue-eyed stranger who, according to Aunt Milly's letter, would soon become her husband. . . .

Shelly scrambled to her feet, hurrying toward the beach. Mark followed.

"You shouldn't look at me like that," she said, her voice soft and bewildered.

"You said it was just a kiss. Was it?"

"Yes," she lied boldly. "How could it be anything more?"

"You tell me."

Shelly had no answers to give him.

"While you're at it, explain why we keep bumping into each other or why I can't stop thinking about you."

"You can't?" She hadn't been able to stop thinking about him, either, but she wasn't ready to admit it.

"No." He stood behind her, his hands caressing her shoulders. Leisurely he stroked the length of her arms. His touch was so light that she thought she was imagining it, and she felt both excited and afraid.

He turned her around and gazed at her lips. "If that was just a run-of-the-mill kiss, then why do I feel the need to do it again?"

"I don't know."

His lips brushed hers. Briefly, with a whisper-soft touch, as though he was testing her response. Shelly closed her eyes and moaned. She didn't want to feel any of this. They were so far apart, such different people. Besides, *he* was involved with another woman and *she* was involved with her career.

When the kiss ended and he slowly released her, it was all Shelly could do to keep from sinking to the sand. "I have . . . to get back to Seattle," she managed to say, backing away from him. She turned and took four or five wobbly steps before she realized she was headed toward the Pacific Ocean.

"Shelly?"

"Yes?"

"Seattle is due north. If you continue going west, you'll eventually end up in Hawaii."

"Oh, yeah, right," she mumbled, reversing her direction, eager now to escape.

The first person Shelly called when she got home was Jill. "Can you come over?" she asked without preamble. She couldn't keep the panic out of her voice.

"Sure. What's wrong?"

"I saw Mark again."

"And?"

"Let me put it like this. We kissed and I haven't stopped trembling since."

Jill's romantic sigh came over the receiver. "This I've got to hear. I'll be there in ten minutes."

Actually it was closer to seven. Shelly had begun pacing the moment she got off the phone. She'd checked her watch repeatedly, waiting desperately for a dose of Jill's good sense.

"Shelly," Jill said, smiling as she breezed into the apartment, "what happened to your hair?"

Shelly smoothed down her curls. "I was at Long Beach."

"That's where you saw Mark? That's kind of a coincidence, isn't it?"

"I saw him earlier in the week, too. . . . Remember I told you I was being audited by the IRS? Lo and behold, guess who was in their waiting room when I arrived?"

"I don't need to be a rocket scientist to figure that one out. Mark Brady!"

"Right." Shelly rubbed her damp palms along her jeans in agitation. They, at least, had finally dried.

"And?"

Shelly groaned. "Can't you see what's

happening? This is the third time we've been thrown together in the past few days. I'd never seen the man before, and all of a sudden he's around every corner. Then the wedding dress fit. It fit you . . . and it fits me."

"I agree that's all rather odd, but I wouldn't put too much stock in it, if I were you."

"Put too much stock in it . . . Listen, Jill, no man's ever made me feel the way Mark does — all weak inside and, I don't know, special somehow. To be perfectly honest, I don't like it." She closed her eyes, hoping to chase away the memory of his touch, but it did no good. "You want to know the real kicker?" she asked abruptly, turning to face her friend. "He's engaged."

"Engaged," Jill echoed, her voice as startled as her expression.

"He keeps insisting it's not official yet. Nevertheless he's involved with someone else."

"But it was you he kissed," Jill pointed out.

"Don't remind me." Shelly covered her eyes with both hands. "I don't mind telling you, I find this whole thing unnerving."

"Obviously. Here," Jill said, directing Shelly toward the kitchen. "Now sit down.

I'll make us some tea, then we can try to reason this out. Honestly, Shell, I don't think I've ever seen you so upset."

"I'm not upset!" she cried. "I'm confused. There's a big difference. I'm . . . I'm trapped." Despite all logic to the contrary, she couldn't help fearing that the entire course of her life was about to change because her aunt Milly had fallen asleep watching *Dr. Phil* one day and had some nonsensical dream.

"Trapped?" Jill said. "Aren't you being a bit dramatic?"

"I don't know anymore." Shelly rested her elbows on the table, buried her face in her hands and breathed in deeply. She had a tendency to become emotional, especially over family issues; she realized that. But this was different. This was scary.

"Calm down," Jill advised. "Once you think it through in a rational manner, you'll realize there's a perfectly ordinary explanation for everything."

Jill's serenity lent Shelly some badly needed confidence. "All right, you explain it."

"I can't," Jill admitted matter-of-factly, pouring boiling water into Shelly's teapot. "I'm not even going to try. My advice to you — once again — is to quit taking all of this so seriously. If a relationship develops between you and Mark, just enjoy it — provided the other woman's out of the picture, of course! But forget about that dress."

"Easy for you to say."

"That's true," Jill agreed. "But you're going to have to do it for your own peace of mind."

Shelly knew good advice when she heard it. "You're right. I'm leaping into the deep end unnecessarily."

"A dress can't make you do anything you don't want to do."

Shelly always counted on her friend's levelheadedness. Although Jill had given her basically the same advice several days earlier, Shelly needed to hear it again.

Jill prepared two cups of tea and carried them to the table. "Are you going to be all right now?"

Shelly nodded. "Of course. I just needed a friend to remind me that I was overreacting." She took a sip of tea, surprised by how much it revived her. "You're still planning to see *Jersey Boys* with me tomorrow afternoon, aren't you?"

The recent Broadway hit was showing locally, and Shelly and Jill had purchased their tickets several weeks earlier.

"That's not tomorrow, is it?" Jill looked stricken, her teacup poised midway to her mouth.

"Jill . . ."

"I promised I'd work for Sharon Belmont. She's got some family thing she has to attend. She was desperate and I completely forgot about the play. Oh, dear, you'll have to go without me."

"You're sure you can't get out of it?" Shelly couldn't help feeling disappointed.

"I'm sure. I'm really sorry, Shell."

Although frustrated that Jill couldn't come with her, Shelly decided to go to the theater alone. She wasn't pleased about it and, given her proclivity for running into Mark Brady, she didn't feel entirely convinced that this wasn't another attempt by the fates to regulate their lives.

However, if she stayed home, she'd be missing a wonderful show. Not only that, she'd be giving in to a nebulous and irrational fear, something she refused to do.

The following afternoon, Shelly dressed carefully, in the type of conservative outfit her mother would have approved of. Mark, too, would approve of her rose-colored linen dress with its matching jacket. . . . The minute the thought flashed through her head, she rejected it.

She was on her way out the door when her phone rang. For a split second she toyed with the idea of not answering. More than likely it was her mother, checking in to see if Shelly had met a prospective husband yet. Her calls had become more frequent and more urgent since Aunt Milly's dress had arrived.

But years of habit prompted her to reach for the phone.

"Shelly." Mark's voice came over the line. "I was about to leave for the afternoon's performance of *Jersey Boys*. Since we seem to have this tendency to run into each other everywhere we go, I thought I should probably clear it with you. If you're going to be there, I'll go another time."

EIGHT

"Actually I was planning to see it this afternoon myself," Shelly admitted hesitantly. "Jill had to cancel at the last minute."

"It seems Janice can't attend, either."

Hearing the other woman's name, the woman Mark loved, had a curious and unexpected effect on Shelly. Her heart sank, and she felt a sharp pang of disappointment. She rebounded quickly, however, forcing a lightness into her voice, a blitheness she didn't feel. "Mark, there's no need for you to miss the show. I'll call the ticket office and see about an exchange."

"No, I will," Mark said.

"That's ridiculous. Jill really wanted to see this musical and —"

"Would it really be so terrible if we both attended the same performance?"

"Uh . . ." The question caught Shelly unprepared. Mark was the one who'd suggested they avoid each other.

"What could it possibly hurt? You have your ticket and I have mine. It'd be absurd to let them go to waste because we're afraid of seeing each other again, don't you think?"

Forming a single, coherent thought seemed beyond Shelly at that moment. After her conversation with Jill the day before, followed by the pep talk she'd given herself, she'd recovered a degree of composure. Now, all of a sudden, she wasn't sure of anything.

"I don't think it should matter," she said finally, although it *did* matter.

"Good. Enjoy the show."

"You, too."

The theater was within walking distance of her apartment building, and Shelly left as soon as she'd finished talking to Mark. He was right. Just because they each had tickets to the same play was no reason for either of them to be penalized.

So Mark was going to see *Jersey Boys.* It wasn't the sort of production she would've thought he'd enjoy. But the man was full of surprises. Riding mopeds on the beach, kissing so spectacularly, and now this . . .

Shelly's mind was full of Mark as she hurried down the steep hill on Cherry Street. The theater was only a block away when she saw him. Her pulse soared and she didn't know if she should smile and wave or simply ignore him.

She didn't need to do either. He stood on the sidewalk, waiting for her.

"You're late," he said, glancing at his watch. "But then you traditionally are." His grin was wide and welcoming. "I can't see any reason not to watch the play together," he went on. "What do you say?"

"You're sure?"

"Positive." He offered her his arm, and she reflected that it was the kind of old-fashioned courtesy she expected from Mark.

The usher seated them and smiled constantly as if to say they were a handsome couple. Shelly was tempted to explain that Mark was engaged to someone else; luckily she managed to hold her tongue. Minutes after they'd settled into their seats, the curtain rose.

The musical was as lively and as good as the reviews claimed, and Shelly enjoyed herself thoroughly. Throughout the performance, however, she was all too aware of Mark sitting next to her. She found herself wondering if he was equally aware of her. She also found herself wondering how long it would be before they "bumped" into each other again — and hoped it was soon.

By the end of the show, Shelly felt inspired

and full of enthusiasm, eager to start a new project of her own. As she and Mark left the theater, she talked excitedly about her idea for the "ocean moods" series. He asked a few questions and even suggested some shots. Before she realized it, they were several blocks past the theater, headed in the opposite direction from her apartment. Shelly paused and glanced around.

"There's an excellent Chinese restaurant in this neighborhood," was all Mark said. Without giving her the opportunity to decline, he gently guided her toward the place he'd mentioned.

It was early for dinner, and they were seated immediately. Although they'd been talking comfortably during their walk, Shelly suddenly felt self-conscious. She played with her linen napkin, smoothing it across her lap.

"I'm not a big fan of musicals, so I hadn't expected to like the show as much as I did," he said after a while.

In that case, Shelly considered it a bit odd that he'd ordered tickets for this production, but perhaps he'd gotten them because Janice had wanted to see *Jersey Boys*.

"It's a little frightening the way we keep running across each other, isn't it?" she ventured.

"I can see how *you'd* find it disconcerting," Mark answered.

"You don't?"

Mark shrugged. "I haven't given it much thought."

"I'll admit all these . . . coincidences do throw me," she said, tracing the outline of a fire-breathing dragon on the menu cover. "But I'm learning to deal with it."

"So you feel you've been caught in something beyond your control?" Mark surprised her by asking.

Shelly lifted her gaze to his, struck by the intensity she read in his eyes. "No, not really. Well . . . a little, maybe. Do you?"

"It wasn't *my* aunt Milly who had the dream."

Shelly smiled and dropped her gaze. "No, but as my friend Jill reminded me recently, no sixty-year-old dress is going to dictate my life. Or yours," she felt obliged to add. Then she understood why he'd asked the question. "You must feel overwhelmed. All of a sudden I've been thrust into your life. There's no escaping me, is there?" she said wryly. "Every time you turn around, there I am."

"Are you going to stand up and tell everyone in the restaurant that you refuse to marry me?"

"No!" Shelly was shocked by his remark until she remembered she'd done exactly that the first time they met.

"If you can resist public declarations, then I think I can bear up under the pressure."

Shelly ignored his mild sarcasm. "I'm not interested in marriage yet," she told him solemnly — just in case he'd forgotten. "I'm satisfied with my life. And I'm too busy for a husband and family."

She hadn't noticed how forcefully she was speaking until she saw several people at other tables glancing in her direction. Instantly she lowered her voice. "Sorry, my views on marriage seem to be more fervent than I realized. But I'm not about to let either my mother or my aunt Milly determine when I decide to settle down and marry."

"Personally, I can't see you ever settling down," Mark said with a small grin. "You don't have to worry. When you're ready, you'll know it."

"Did you?" She hadn't meant to bring up Janice, but it seemed wise to remind him — and her — that there was someone else in his life.

Mark raised one shoulder casually. "More or less. I took a good, long look at my life and discovered I'd already achieved several of my professional goals. It was time to invest my energy in developing the personal aspects — marriage, children and the like."

Mark talked about marriage as if it were the next chapter in a book he was reading or part of a connect-the-dots picture. Shelly couldn't stop herself from frowning.

"You have a problem with that?"

"Not a problem, exactly. I happen to think of marriage a bit differently, that's all."

"In what way?"

He seemed genuinely interested, otherwise she would've kept her opinions to herself. "People should fall in love," she said slowly. "I don't think it's necessary or even possible to plan for that. Love can be unexpected — it can take a couple by surprise, knock them both off their feet."

"You make falling in love sound like an accident — like tripping on the stairs or something."

Shelly smiled. "In some ways, I think that's how it should be. Marriage is one of the most important decisions in anyone's life, so it should be a *deeply felt* decision. It should feel inevitable. It's the union of two lives, after all. So you can't simply check your watch and announce 'it's time.' " She was suddenly concerned that she'd spoken out of turn and might have offended him, but one quick glance assured her that wasn't the case.

Mark leaned forward. "I would never have guessed it," he said.

"Guessed what?" She was beginning to feel a little foolish now.

"That a woman who gives the impression of being a scatterbrain is really quite reflective. Beneath those glow-in-the-dark sweatshirts lies a very romantic heart."

"I seem to get emotional about certain things," she responded, studying the menu, eager to change the subject. "I really like hot-and-sour soup. Have you ever tried it?"

Their conversation over dinner remained light and amusing. Shelly noticed that Mark avoided any more discussion of a personal nature, as did she.

After they'd finished their dinner and Mark had paid the bill, they strolled leisurely back toward the theater. Mark offered to drive her home when they reached his parked car, but Shelly declined. Her apartment was only a couple of blocks north and she preferred to walk.

Walk and think. Their time together had given her plenty to think about.

"Thank you for dinner," she said as he unlocked the car.

"You're welcome," he answered. "Well,

good night for now," he said, grinning. "I suspect I'll be seeing you soon."

She grinned back. "Probably within a day or two. Maybe we should synchronize our schedules," she teased.

"That wouldn't bother you, would it? If we ran into each other, I mean."

"Oh, no. What about you?" She hated the way her voice rose expectantly with the question. She certainly wasn't *bothered* by the prospect of seeing him again. In fact, she was downright eager to see what tricks fate would play on them next.

Mark's eyes found hers then, and he slowly pocketed his car keys. His look was so potent, so full of emotion, that Shelly took a step in retreat. "I had a wonderful afternoon, a wonderful evening. Thanks again," she said nervously.

Mark didn't say a word as he continued to gaze at her.

"The play was great, wasn't it? And dinner . . . fabulous." Shelly's throat seemed to close as Mark stepped onto the curb and walked toward her.

The whole world came to an abrupt halt when she realized he intended to kiss her. *Not again,* her mind shouted. *Please hurry,* her heart sang.

Her heart tripped wildly as Mark lowered

his head, his mouth seeking hers. Despite the fierce battle inside her, Shelly had to admit how much she wanted this kiss. If for no other reason, she told herself, than to prove that the first time had been a fluke.

Only it happened again. But this kiss was a hundred times more compelling than the first one they'd shared. A hundred times more exciting.

Shelly wanted to cry out at the unfairness of it all. If a man's kiss was going to affect her like this, why did it have to be Mark Brady's?

He broke away from her reluctantly, his warm breath fanning her cheek. His eyes were filled with questions, filled with surprise. Shelly wasn't sure what her own eyes were saying to him. She didn't even want to know.

"Take care," he whispered as he turned away.

Shelly stayed home from work on Monday. She wasn't sick, just puzzled and confused. Nothing about her relationship with Mark made sense. He was everything she *didn't* want in a man — and everything she did.

Shelly didn't realize how despondent she was until she found herself standing barefoot in front of her closet, carrying on a conversation with Aunt Milly's wedding dress.

"I'll have you know I had a perfectly good life until you got here," she muttered. "Now my whole world's been turned upside down." She slammed the door shut, then jerked it open. "No wonder Mrs. Livingston's cat wouldn't go near you. You're *dangerous.*"

NINE

"The show was great," Shelly told Jill over coffee Wednesday afternoon. She'd stopped off at PayRite, hoping Jill could get away for lunch. "Even Mark —"

"Mark?" Jill's coffee cup hit the saucer with a clang. "He went to see *Jersey Boys*?"

Shelly nodded sheepishly. "I guess I forgot to mention I ran into him, didn't I? Actually he called me first and since we both had plans to attend the same performance, we decided to go together."

"Is there anything else you haven't told me?" Jill's eyes narrowed astutely.

Shelly tried to hide her uneasiness behind a relaxed shrug, but how well she succeeded in fooling Jill remained to be seen. "We had dinner afterward . . . as friends. It didn't mean anything. I did tell you he's engaged, didn't I?"

"*Unofficially* engaged." Jill was studying her closely and Shelly felt uneasy under her scrutiny.

"We've been friends for a long time," Jill reminded her. "I know you, and I know there's something troubling you."

Shelly nodded. There was no point in hiding the truth from Jill. Her need to confide in a sympathetic, understanding person was the very reason for her impromptu visit to Jill's workplace. Lunch had been a convenient excuse.

"You won't believe this," Shelly said, cradling the coffee cup in both hands and keeping her gaze lowered. "I can hardly believe it myself."

"You're falling in love with Mark."

Shelly's eyes shot upward. "It's that obvious?"

"No," Jill said softly. "But you look like you're about to break into tears."

"If I wasn't so darn irritated I would. Good grief, think about it. Can you imagine two people less suited to each other? Mark is so . . . so responsible . . ."

"So are you."

"Not in the same way," Shelly argued. "He's so sincere and —"

"Shelly, so are you."

"Perhaps, but I'm such a scatterbrain." She grimaced as she remembered that was the very word Mark had used. "I'm disorganized and always late and I like to do things my own way. You know that better than most."

"I prefer to think of you as creative."

Shelly sent Jill a smile of appreciation. "That's the reason you're my best friend. I don't mind telling you, Jill, I'm worried. Mark Brady may be the Rock of Gibraltar, but I doubt he's got an original thought in his head. Everything's done by the book or according to a schedule."

"You need someone like Mark in your life," Jill returned. "Don't look so shocked. It's true. The two of you balance each other. He needs you because you're fun and crazy and imaginative, and you need him because he knows his multiplication tables by heart and will remind you when it's time for meals."

"The problem is, Mark's the type of man who'd expect a woman to *cook* those meals."

Jill chuckled.

"If the fates are determined to match me up with a man," Shelly moaned, "couldn't it be with someone other than an accountant?"

"Apparently not."

"What really angers me is that I allowed it to happen. The first time he kissed me —"

"He *kissed* you?" Jill feigned a look of horror.

Shelly ignored it. "Yes. Twice. It's only natural — our being curious about each other, don't you think?"

"I suppose," Jill said quickly, no longer teasing. "So tell me what happened."

"Fireworks bigger than the Fourth of July. I've never experienced the feelings I do with Mark, and all because of a kiss." She paused. "Well, two kisses."

"And does Mark feel the same thing?"

"I — I can't speak for him, but I assume it's equally disturbing for him. He certainly looked as if he'd been taken by surprise."

"How do you get along with him otherwise?"

"Fine, I guess." Shelly took a sip of her coffee. "I'm sure I amuse him. But someone like Mark isn't looking for a woman to entertain him, any more than I'm looking for a man to handle my finances."

"His opinion of you has mellowed, hasn't it?" Jill asked, then answered her own question. "There was a time when he thought you were more than a little bizarre, remember?"

Shelly did, all too well. "At first I thought he was totally unexciting, but I've altered my opinion of him, too."

106

"So what's the problem?"

"I don't *want* to fall in love," Shelly said pointedly. "I've got bigger plans for my life than to tie myself down to a committed relationship right now."

"Then don't. It shouldn't be that difficult. Decide what you want and disregard everything else. There's no law that says you have to fall in love this minute. For that matter, no one can regulate when and who you marry, either. Not even your aunt Milly."

Jill was saying everything Shelly wanted to hear. Everything she *needed* to hear. But it didn't make any difference; her heart was already involved. If she could forget she'd ever met Mark, she would. But it was too late. She was in love with him. With Mark, who was in love with someone else. Mark, who saw love and marriage as goals to be achieved within a certain time frame. He'd probably never done anything impulsive in his life.

A relationship between them would never last. If he wasn't smart enough to figure that out, she was. Something had to be done and soon, and Shelly knew it would be up to her to do it.

Shelly didn't have long to wait before she saw Mark again. They met at the main branch of the Seattle Public Library on Wednesday evening. She was returning ten overdue books. Six months overdue. The library had sent her three warnings, each progressively less friendly.

She was half-afraid the buzzer inside the library entrance would go off the moment she walked through the hallowed doors, and armed officers would haul her away.

"I wondered when we'd find each other again," Mark said, strolling up to her at the counter. She'd seen him almost immediately and tried to pretend she hadn't.

Shelly acknowledged him with a quick nod and ordered her heart to be still. She managed a slight smile. "Hello again," she said, drawing a checkbook out of her purse. At least she'd come prepared. The fine for the books was sure to be monstrous; in fact, it might be cheaper to buy them.

Mark set the two volumes he was borrowing on the counter. Shelly noted the titles — *Tools for Time Management* and *The State of the Language,* and groaned inwardly. To someone like her accountant friend, these books were probably easy reading. Her own tastes leaned more toward mystery and romance, with a little nonfiction thrown in.

"Have you got time for a cup of coffee?" Mark asked as she wrote out the check to pay her fine.

She was gladdened by the invitation, but knew she had to refuse it. Before he could say or do anything to change her mind, she shook her head. "Not tonight, thanks."

His smile faded as though her refusal had startled him. "You're busy?"

She nodded, smiling at the librarian as she handed over her check. The librarian smiled back. It had been a civilized exchange, Shelly thought, and her library card had't been confiscated, despite her transgressions.

"You've got a date waiting for you?"

It took Shelly a second to understand that Mark was referring to her refusal to join him for coffee.

"Not exactly." She turned away from the counter and headed toward the exit. To her surprise Mark followed her outside.

"Something's wrong," he said, standing at the top of the steps.

She stopped her descent and stood below him, looking up. Pretense had never suited Shelly; she was too innately honest to hide her feelings. "Mark, I think you're a very nice man —"

"But you don't want to marry me," he concluded for her. "I've heard that line before, remember? Actually, half the mall heard it, too."

"I've already apologized for that. It's just that . . . all right, if you must know, I'm beginning to like you . . . really like you, and frankly that terrifies me."

Her candid response seemed to unnerve him. He frowned and rubbed the side of his jaw. "I know what you mean. I'm beginning to like you, too."

"See!" she cried, raising both hands. "If we don't take care of this now, heaven only knows what could happen. It has the potential of ruining both our lives. We're mature adults, aren't we?" At the moment, though, she felt singularly lacking in maturity.

All her senses were clamoring, telling her to enjoy their brief time together, despite the consequences. It was what her heart wanted, but she couldn't allow her life to be ruled by her heart. Not when it came to Mark.

"Liking each other doesn't have to be a federal crime," he said, advancing one step toward her.

"You're right, of course, but I know myself too well. I could easily fall in love with you, Mark." She didn't dare admit she already had. "Before we knew it, we'd be spending more and more time with each other. We might even become seriously involved."

He remained suspiciously silent.

"You're a wonderful man. If my mother were to meet you she'd be shouting from the rooftops, she'd be so thrilled. For a while I might convince myself that we could really make something of this relationship. I might even consider taking cooking classes because you're the kind of man who'd expect a woman to know how to make a roast and mashed potatoes."

"It'd probably come in handy someday," he said.

"That's what I thought," she murmured, disheartened. "I'm not a traditional woman. I never will be. The only time I ever baked a pie I ended up throwing it in the garbage disposal — and it broke the disposal."

"A pie ruined your garbage disposal?" Mark repeated, then shook his head. "Never mind, don't bother explaining. It seems to me you're getting ahead of yourself here. You're talking as though coffee together means a lifetime commitment."

Shelly wasn't listening. "What about Janice?" she demanded. "*She's* the one you should be inviting to coffee, not me."

"What's Janice got to do with this?" he asked impatiently.

"Janice," Shelly snapped, her own temper short. "The woman you've decided to marry. Remember her? The love of your life? The woman you're unofficially engaged to marry."

"It's not unofficial anymore," Mark explained evenly.

"Oh, great, you're taking me out to dinner, kissing me and at the same time picking out engagement rings with another woman." She had to admit he'd never lied to her about his relationship with the faceless Janice. He'd been forthright about it from the beginning. But it hurt, really hurt, to learn that he was going ahead with his plans to marry Janice.

He was about to speak, but she forestalled him, struggling to force some enthusiasm into her voice. "Congratulations are in order. I wish you both the very best." With that she turned and bounded down the stairs, taking them recklessly fast.

"Shelly!"

She could hear Mark calling after her, but she ignored him, desperate to get away before the lump in her throat made it impossible to breathe. Tears had formed in her eyes and she cursed herself for being so ridiculous, for caring so much. Her vision blurred and she wiped a hand across her face, furious at her lack of control. This marriage was what she'd hoped would happen. What she wanted for Mark. *Wasn't it?*

"Shelly, for heaven's sake, will you wait?"

When she reached the bottom of the steps, Shelly moved into a side street, hoping to disappear in the crowd, praying Mark wouldn't pursue her.

She thought she'd escaped until a hand on her shoulder whirled her around.

"Shelly, please listen," Mark pleaded breathlessly, his shoulders heaving. "The engagement isn't official because there is no engagement. How could I possibly marry Janice after meeting you?"

TEN

"You broke off your engagement with Janice?" Shelly demanded furiously. Something inside, some reservoir of emotion, had burst wide-open. "You fool," she shouted. "You idiot!" Her eyes brimmed with tears, and deep in her heart she felt the stirrings of glad excitement. "That was the worst thing you could've done!"

"No," he said. "It was the smartest."

"How can you say that?" she wailed.

"Shelly?"

He reached for her as though to offer comfort, but Shelly jerked away and stepped back, freeing herself from his grasp. "Janice was perfect for you," she lamented.

"How do you know that?" he asked calmly and much too reasonably to suit Shelly. "You never met her."

"I didn't need to. I know she was right for you. You'd never have asked her to marry you if she wasn't."

"Janice is a wonderful woman and she'll make some man a good wife, but it won't be me."

"You're crazy to break off your engagement. Crazy!"

"No, I'm not," Mark returned confidently. "I'm absolutely certain I did the right thing. Do you know why?"

Shelly could only shake her head, wiping away the tears with the back of her hand. She was ecstatic — and yet she was so frightened. She loved him; she was sure of it. Then why had everything become so difficult and confused?

"What you said about love the other day changed my mind."

"You *listened* to me?" she cried in real horror. "Do I look like an expert on love? I've never been in love in my life!" Not counting what she felt for him, of course. She'd always thought love would clarify her life, not make it more complicated.

Mark paid no attention to her outburst. "You helped me understand that I was marrying Janice for the wrong reasons. I'd decided it was time to settle down. Janice had come to the same conclusion. She's thirty and figured if she was going to marry and have a family, the time was now. It wasn't a love match, and we both knew it."

"This is none of my business," Shelly said, frantically shaking her head as if to chase the words away. "I don't want to hear it."

"You *are* going to hear it," Mark insisted, clasping her elbows and gently drawing her closer. "You claimed people shouldn't plan love. It should take them by surprise, you said, and you were right. Janice and I are fond of each other, but —"

"There's nothing wrong with fond!"

His eyes widened. "No, there isn't," he agreed, "but Janice isn't a zany producer. I like spending time with you. I've come to realize there's a certain thrill in expecting the unexpected. Every minute with you is an adventure."

"A relationship between us would never last," Shelly insisted, drawing on the most sensible argument. "It would be fine for a while, but then we'd drift apart. We'd have to. In case you haven't noticed, we're nothing alike."

"Why wouldn't a relationship last?" Mark asked patiently.

"For all the reasons I listed before!" Mark was so endearing, and he was saying all the words she'd secretly longed to hear, but nothing could change the fundamental differences between them.

"So you aren't as adept in the kitchen as

some women. I'm a fair cook."

"It's more than that."

"Of course it is," he concurred. "But there's nothing we can't overcome if we're willing to work together."

"You know what I think it is?" she said desperately, running her splayed fingers through her hair. "You're beginning to believe there's magic in Aunt Milly's wedding dress."

"Don't you?"

"No," she cried. "Not anymore. I did when I was a little girl . . . I loved the story of how Aunt Milly met Uncle John, but I'm not a child anymore, and what seemed so romantic then just seems unrealistic now."

"Shelly," Mark said in exasperation. "We don't need to do anything right away. All I'm suggesting is we give this thing between us a chance."

"There's nothing between us," she denied vehemently.

Mark's eyes narrowed. "You don't honestly believe that, do you?"

"Yes," she lied. "You're a nice guy, but —"

"If I hear any more of this nice-guy stuff I'm going to kiss you and we both know what'll happen then."

His gaze lowered to her mouth and she

unconsciously moistened her lips with anticipation.

"I just might, anyway."

"No." The threat was real enough to make her retreat a couple of steps. If Mark kissed her, Shelly knew she'd be listening to her heart and not her head. And then *he'd* know . . . "That's what I thought." His grin was downright boyish.

"I think we should both forget we ever met," she suggested next, aware even as she said it how ludicrous she sounded. Mark Brady had indelibly marked her life and no matter how much she denied it, she'd never forget him.

"Don't you remember that you threw yourself into my arms? *You* can conveniently choose to overlook the obvious, but unfortunately that won't work for me. I'm falling in love with you, Shelly."

She opened her mouth to argue that he couldn't possibly love her — not yet, not on such short acquaintance — but he pressed his finger to her lips, silencing her.

"At first I wasn't keen on the idea," he admitted, "but it's sort of grown on me since. I can see us ten years in the future and you know what? It's a pleasant picture. We're going to be very happy together."

"I need to think!" She placed her hands

on either side of her head. Everything was happening much too quickly; she actually felt dizzy. "We'll leave it to fate . . . how does that sound?" she offered excitedly. It seemed like the perfect solution. "The next time we bump into each other, I'll have more of a grasp on my feelings. I'll know what we should do." She might also hibernate inside her apartment for a month, but she wasn't mentioning that.

"Nope." Mark slowly shook his head. "That won't work."

"Why not?" she asked. "We bump into each other practically every day."

"No, we don't."

He wasn't making any sense.

"*Jersey Boys* was a setup," he informed her. "I made sure we bumped into each other there."

"How? When?"

"The day at the beach I saw the ticket sticking out of your purse. Our meeting at the theater wasn't any accident."

Mark couldn't have shocked her more if he'd announced he was an alien from outer space. For the first time in recent memory, she was left speechless. "Tonight?" she asked when she could get the words out. "The library?"

"I'd decided to stop off at your apartment.

I was prepared to make up some story about the wedding dress luring me into your building, but when I drove past, I saw you coming down the front steps loaded down with library books. It wasn't hard to figure out where you were headed. I found a parking space and waited for you inside."

"What about . . . the IRS office and the beach?" She didn't know how he'd managed *those* meetings.

Mark shook his head again and grinned. "Coincidence, unless you had anything to do with them. You didn't, did you?"

"Absolutely not," she replied indignantly.

Still grinning, he said, "I didn't really think you had."

Shelly started walking, her destination unclear. She felt too restless to continue standing there; unfortunately the one action that truly appealed to her was leaping into his arms.

Mark matched his own steps to hers.

"It's Aunt Milly's wedding dress, I know it is," Shelly mumbled under her breath. She'd tried to bring up the subject, but Mark had refused to listen. "You broke off an engagement because you believe fate's somehow thrown us together."

"No, Shelly, the dress doesn't have anything to do with how I feel," Mark said calmly.

"But you'd already decided to marry someone else!"

"I'm choosing my own destiny, which is to spend the rest of my life with you."

"You might have consulted me first. I have no intention of getting married . . . not for years and years."

"I'll wait."

"You can't do that," she cried. He didn't understand because he was too respectable and adorable and too much of a gentleman. The only thing that would work would be to heartlessly send him away.

She faced Mark, careful to wear just the right expression of remorse and regret. "This is all very flattering, but I don't love you. I'm sorry, Mark. You're the last person in the world I want to hurt."

For a moment Mark said nothing, then he shrugged and looked away. "You can't be any more direct than that, can you? There's no chance you'll ever fall in love with me?"

"None." Her breath fell harshly, painfully, from her lips. It shouldn't hurt this much to do the right thing. It shouldn't hurt to be noble. "You're very nice, but . . ."

"So you've said before."

Falteringly, as though the movement

caused him pain, he lifted his hand to her face, his fingers caressing the curve of her jaw.

Until that moment, Shelly hadn't understood how fiercely proud Mark was. He could have dealt with every argument, calmed every doubt, answered every question, but there was nothing he could say when she denied all feeling for him.

"You mean it, don't you?" he asked huskily. He was standing so close that his breath warmed her face.

Shelly had schooled her features to reveal none of her clamoring emotions. His touch, so light, so potent, seemed to clog her throat with anguish, and she couldn't speak.

"If that's what you want —" he dropped his hand abruptly "— I won't trouble you again." With those words, he turned and walked away. Before she fully realized what he intended, Mark had disappeared around a corner.

"You let him go, you idiot!" she whispered to herself. A tear escaped and she smeared it across her cheek.

Mark meant what he'd said about not bothering her. He was a man of his word. He'd never try to see her again — and if they did happen upon each other, he'd pretend he didn't know her.

He might eventually decide to marry Janice. Hadn't he admitted he was fond of the other woman?

Shelly's heart clutched painfully inside her chest. Before she could stop herself, before she could question the wisdom of her actions, she ran after Mark.

She turned the corner and was halfway down the block when she realized he wasn't anywhere to be seen. She came to a skidding halt, then whirled around, wondering how he could possibly have gotten so far in such a short time.

Mark stepped out from the side of a building, hands on his hips, a cocky, jubilant smile on his face. "What took you so long?" he asked, holding out his arms.

Shelly didn't need a second invitation to throw herself into his embrace. His mouth feasted on hers, his kiss hungry and demanding, filled with enough emotion to last a lifetime.

Shelly slid her arms around his neck and stood on her tiptoes, giving herself completely to his kiss, to his love. All that mattered was being in his arms — exactly where she was supposed to be.

"I take it this means you love me, too?" he whispered close to her ear. His voice was rough with emotion.

Shelly nodded. "I'm so afraid."

"Don't be. I'm confident enough for both of us."

"This is crazy," she said, but she couldn't have moved out of his arms for the world. Breathing deeply, she buried her face in his chest.

"But it's a good kind of crazy."

"Aunt Milly saw us together in her dream. She wrote to me about a tall, blue-eyed man."

"Who knows if it was me or not?" Mark whispered into her hair and brushed his lips over her temple. "Who cares? If fate had anything to do with me finding you or if your aunt Milly's wedding dress is responsible, I can't say. Personally, I couldn't care less. I love you, Shelly, and I believe you love me, too."

She glanced up at this man who had altered the course of her life and smiled, her heart too full for words. "I do love you," she said when she could. "An accountant! In a suit! Hardly the husband I imagined for myself."

Mark chuckled. "I would never have guessed I'd fall head over heels in love with a woman who wears the type of clothes you do — but I did."

"I love you, too," Shelly said and closed

her eyes.

The morning of her wedding day, Shelly couldn't sit still. Her mother was even worse, pacing in front of her, dabbing her eyes and sniffling.

"I can't believe my baby's getting married."

Shelly had to restrain herself from reminding her dear mother that less than a month before, she'd been desperate to marry her daughter off. Thank goodness Jill was there. Without her best friend to reassure her, Shelly didn't know what she would've done. While her mother fussed with the caterers, complained to the florists and fretted about who had a key to the kitchen in the reception hall, Jill led Shelly upstairs to her childhood bedroom and helped her dress. When Shelly was finished, Jill stood back to examine her.

"Well?" Shelly asked, smoothing her hand down the antique dress, loving the feel of the satin and lace against her fingers. It was probably her imagination but now that she was wearing the dress, really wearing it, she could almost feel its magic.

Tears gathered in Jill's eyes as she stared at her friend.

"That bad?" Shelly teased.

Jill pressed her fingers to her lips. "You're beautiful," she whispered. "Mark isn't going to believe his eyes when he sees you."

"Do you really think so?" Shelly hated sounding so insecure, but she wanted everything to be perfect today. She was crazy in love — and crazy enough to give her mother free rein planning her wedding. Crazy enough to go through with a formal wedding in the first place. If it'd been up to her, they would've eloped weeks ago. But Mark had wanted a proper wedding and her mother certainly wasn't going to be cheated out of this moment. So Shelly had gone along with it.

Mark and her mother had defeated most of her ideas. She'd wanted to hire clowns to entertain at the reception, but her mother didn't seem to think that was a good idea.

Shelly had never been that fond of white wedding cake, either. She'd suggested Cherries Jubilee instead, but Mark was afraid something might catch on fire and so in the interests of safety, Shelly had agreed to a traditional cake, decorated with pink roses.

A knock sounded on her bedroom door and Jill opened it. In walked Aunt Milly, looking absolutely delighted with herself.

She introduced herself to Jill, then turned to gaze lovingly at Shelly. "So I see the dress worked."

"It worked," Shelly agreed.

"You love him?"

Shelly nodded. "Enough to eat white wedding cake."

Milly laughed softly and sat on the edge of the bed. Her hair was gray and her face wrinkled, but her eyes were still blue and clear. It was difficult to tell that she was a woman well into her eighties. She clasped both of Shelly's hands in her own.

"Nervous?"

Shelly nodded again.

"I was, too, although I knew to the bottom of my heart that I'd made the right decision in marrying John."

"I feel the same way about Mark."

Aunt Milly hugged her tightly. "You're going to be very happy, my dear."

An hour later Shelly and Mark stood at the front of a packed church with Pastor Johnson, who'd known her most of her life. He smiled warmly as he spoke a few words, then asked Shelly to repeat her vows.

Linking hands with Mark, she raised her eyes to his. Everyone else faded away. Aunt Milly. Jill. Her mother. Her long-suffering dad. Her brothers and their wives. There were only the two of them. She felt a jolt of pure joy at the love that radiated from Mark's eyes. He stood tall and proud, his gaze holding hers, the love shining through without question, shining through for her to read. Shelly knew her eyes told him the same thing.

Later, Shelly couldn't remember speaking her vows, although she was sure she did. The words came directly from her heart. Directly from Mark's.

They'd been drawn to this place and this time by forces neither fully understood. Shelly wasn't entirely sure she believed Aunt Milly's wedding dress was responsible, but as Mark had said, it didn't matter. They were there out of love. She didn't know exactly when it had happened. Perhaps that day on the beach, when Mark first kissed her. Something had happened then, something that touched them both.

The love that began as a small spark had grown and flared to life until they'd been brought here, to stand before God and family, pledging their lives to each other.

To love. To cherish. All the days of their lives.

ABOUT THE AUTHOR

Debbie Macomber is a number one *New York Times* bestselling author. Her recent books include *92 Pacific Boulevard, 8 Sandpiper Way, 74 Seaside Avenue* and *Debbie Macomber's Cedar Cove Cookbook* as well as *Twenty Wishes, A Cedar Cove Christmas, Summer on Blossom Street* and *The Perfect Christmas.* She has become a leading voice in women's fiction worldwide and her work has appeared on every major bestseller list, including those of the *New York Times, USA TODAY, Publishers Weekly* and *Entertainment Weekly.* She is a multiple award winner, and she won the 2005 Quill Award for Best Romance. There are more than 100 million copies of her books in print. For more information on Debbie and her books, visit her Web site, www.DebbieMacomber.com.

We hope you have enjoyed this Large Print book. Other Thorndike, Wheeler, Kennebec, and Chivers Press Large Print books are available at your library or directly from the publishers.

For information about current and upcoming titles, please call or write, without obligation, to:

Publisher
Thorndike Press
295 Kennedy Memorial Drive
Waterville, ME 04901
Tel. (800) 223-1244

or visit our Web site at:

http://gale.cengage.com/thorndike

OR

Chivers Large Print
published by BBC Audiobooks Ltd
St James House, The Square
Lower Bristol Road
Bath BA2 3SB
England
Tel. +44(0) 800 136919
email: bbcaudiobooks@bbc.co.uk
www.bbcaudiobooks.co.uk

All our Large Print titles are designed for easy reading, and all our books are made to last.